Magic Words in the Palace of Desire

lou zitnik

Hilo, Hawai'i

ISBN: 978-0-6152-3950-7
Library of Congress Control Number: 2001012345

Printed in the United States of America.

PUBLISHER'S NOTE

This is a work of fiction. Names, characters, places, and
incidents either are the product of the author's imagination
or are used fictitiously, and any resemblance to actual
persons, living or dead, business establishments, events, or
locales is entirely coincidental.

ALOHA

Cover design and photos by lou zitnik. Photos of lou and
cats on page 252 by Amy Self. For more information about
this novel or other work by lou, visit his website:
louzitnik.com

Acknowledgements

Many thanks and good memories to
Amy Self, Patsy and Ernesto.

Chapter 1

Patsy inhaled the salty scent of tears, looked up, pressed her paws against the cold floor, and jumped. A second later, she landed on the table, front claws digging into a message written across Humphrey Bogart's face.

> dear steamer,
> you're a good man and i love you,
> so please understand. i have to go.
> someday soon we'll be together. i promise.
> please understand. and please, please
> take care of the cats!
> love always,
> mimi

Staring at the words, Patsy struggled to understand their meaning. She tried each word by itself, all of them together, some upside down. But her efforts produced only a quickly fading memory of the woman walking in the green and yellow glow of the Palace's neon sign, stopping to say, "Don't worry. Steamer will take care of you."

Then she was gone.

Patsy looked at the camera, the empty closet, and the woman's rubber slippers. Where was she now? Did the man know when she would return? Like a cat, he was not good with words. This morning he had sat here acting as if he were seeing them for the first time, staring at them as if the longer he stared the more likely their secret would be revealed. When that failed, he brushed the dusty cookie crumbs off the poster, and did what a cat would do. He closed his eyes, and pressed his lips to the blue ink.

Patsy knew that much more could be learned by smelling and tasting than by staring and thinking. She sniffed the paper's worn edges, inhaled the scent of chocolate and tears. She licked each letter of the note, tasted the numbing flavor of blue ink. The woman was not here. That much was certain. In her place, something sharp and heavy was moving toward the Palace.

When the table shook, Patsy jumped to the floor and ran out the bedroom door, through the projection booth and into the balcony. She found Steamer sitting alone in the shadowy darkness, watching a flat man and a flat woman struggle to reach each other. Unlike Steamer, they seemed aware of the danger that had passed underneath them. They waved, called out, and struggled against a surging mob as it swept them toward a black train. The man stretched out his hand. The woman reached for him. They touched, held and embraced, growing larger and larger until their faces filled the screen.

"Kiss her," Steamer whispered. Their lips almost touched. "Hold her. Don't let her go."

Patsy did not know why Steamer bothered to offer these words of advice. Flat people did not listen. They did what they did no matter what people in the Palace yelled at them. Steamer knew this, had seen it happen a hundred times, so what made him think that this train couple was any different?

She shook her collar to draw his attention away from the screen. How long had he been sitting here, hoping for something that would never happen? She watched him reach down, and felt his hand on her neck. Two strong fingers dug under her collar.

"Got to start eating," he said. "Your collar's getting loose."

The train whistle sounded as raindrops fell on black umbrellas. The crowd swirled, gathered its strength, and before the couple could kiss broke them apart. The woman was swept back, left at a gate in a circle of light, the man carried away to a train puffing dark smoke. Men in uniform, rifles strapped to their shoulders, lifted him aboard as he called out to her, his words lost in the train's roar.

"Love," Steamer whispered.

Suddenly, like magic, the train did something it had never done before. Instead of rushing the men off to certain death, it puffed its way into a swirling cloud that faded into a hospital room. The man was lying in bed, his eyes closed and his breathing a whisper. The nurse, the same woman who a moment ago had been struggling to reach the train, held the man's hand as a doctor said, "I'm afraid there's nothing we can do."

As soon as the doctor left the room, the woman bent over the dying man, kissed him on the lips, and whispered, "I love you."

The two of them were instantly, magically, transported out of the hospital and onto a smooth stretch of sandy white beach where sweet music flowed over rolling waves. They pointed at the horizon, where, as the sun descended into a deep blue sea, something in the distance was moving toward them.

Patsy watched the screen with new interest. If the flat humans and Steamer could use these magic words to perform miracles, could she use them to bring Mimi home?

Turning to Steamer, she saw a tear on his cheek. She felt her heart beat faster, tried to shape the magic words with her mouth but managed only an extended squeak. Barely a sound.

On the torn screen, the happy couple dissolved into a mass of charging men, violent explosions, and tortured screams. Eyes open, arms waving, the man who seconds ago had been walking into the sunset with his magical nurse was lifted into the air and thrown against a barbwire fence. His screaming face filled the giant screen.

Patsy ran. Like Mimi, she did not like loud noises. She left Steamer in the darkness and hurried down the aisle, past rows of empty seats. The closer she got to the flat people, the more they retreated, until they dissolved into splashes of see-through color and bright light. Below them, at the back of the orchestra pit, in the narrow space behind the organ, she found Ernesto curled up in an abandoned violin case, his favorite sleeping spot.

She stared at him, willing him to wake, so close to his tiny grey nose that she could smell his dreams of sticky rice and skillet fried ahi. She sniffed his head, his neck, and found the delicate scent of night-blooming jasmine. How long ago had the woman rubbed her hands through his grey fur? Mimi, she thought, exhaling the delicate scent of memories in his tiny ear. Love.

Magically, Ernie's eyes blinked wide open. He yawned, and when his mouth snapped shut, Patsy darted away, glanced back, saw him lick his paw, rub his eye, and stretch.

Slipping behind the curtain, Patsy let the white tip of her tail linger. Even though he did not know the ending of the chase game, he was good at the beginning. Quick and agile but slow to start, he would follow. She shook her collar, waited a second, shook it again, then hurried down the stairs. He knew the way, had chased her down these steps many times. She stopped at the door Mimi had cut for her in the corrugated iron and heard her say,

"When there's no other way. You know what I mean?"

Patsy did not know. She was not good with words, but she liked the door. She ducked through the hole, careful not to scrape her back on the sharp edge.

Sunlight and misty rain fell on the narrow alley. She avoided the dangling pieces of the rusty fire escape and stepped onto the wet concrete. Walking slowly, avoiding puddles, she brushed along the smooth skin of the Palace. Searching for the scent of jasmine, she slipped by an abandoned popcorn machine, stepped over a broken row of theater seats, and stopped at an overstuffed dumpster. It smelled of milk and mildew and something else, something dangerous.

She looked back. No Ernie, but she was not worried. With his extra long legs, misty grey hair, and super thin body, he could run faster than almost any cat in Hilo. She was faster, but as long as she did not go far from the Palace, he would find her, and together they would find the woman.

Across the alley, sunlight stretched over Mr. Goodmorning's building, circled in from the street, touched the wet concrete.

Stepping behind the dumpster, Patsy found Angelica the Calico sleeping in a cardboard box next to the drainpipe. Last night, Patsy had passed this way and seen Angelica sleeping alone. Now she had her head on the drainpipe while a line of kittens nibbled at her breasts. Patsy counted six of them, no, seven. Someone had lined the box with old newspapers and left two bowls, one for food and one for water, next to the box. The food bowl was empty except for a few broken bits of industrial strength tuna treats. A coqui frog foot floated in the shallow water.

Patsy crept close to a tiny orange female that had slipped from Angelica's breast. Number seven. She smelled its neck, its milky sweet breath, and licked glistening raindrops off its back.

I love you, she thought as the kitten's tiny mouth pressed against her fur. I love you. She felt her nipples tingle. Through half-open eyes, she saw clouds moving across the sky. The morning light faded, grew bright. A soft breeze carried the salty smell of ocean and rust and roasted chicken.

Ears back, Patsy pushed the kitten toward her mother's breast. The other kittens did not budge. Like Ernie often was, they were too busy eating to notice any danger.

From a window two flights up, a raspy voice shouted, "Good morning, neighbors!"

Somewhere far off, a dog barked.

Patsy darted to the nearest shadow, looked up to see Mr. Goodmorning, tall and wiry, leaning out of his third-story window and waving at her. "You be careful down there, girl!" he shouted, pointing at the dumpster.

A beer bottle slid down a pile of garbage, bounced off rusting metal, and shattered against concrete. At the lip of the dumpster, Rusty appeared, growing bigger as he leaned toward her, studying her with green eyes.

Patsy rubbed slowly along the corrugated tin of the Palace. She stopped and turned back toward the dumpster, waving the white spot at the tip of her tail. She did not know why she did these things. She did them without thinking. Rusty was big, almost twice the size of Ernie, with teeth sharp enough to bite into a Pit Bull, but Patsy did not fear him. She waited for him.

His front paws landed first, then his back, light and heavy. He looked at Patsy, at Angelica, at the small orange kitten struggling to reach its mother's breast.

Love, Patsy tried to whisper. Love.

He leaned forward, opened his mouth, baring sharp fangs, and bit into the kitten's tiny neck.

Patsy threw her weight into him, knocked him back against the drainpipe. As she turned to run, she felt his paws on her, then his sharp teeth digging into her neck, pressing her into the slippery asphalt, into the heavy smell of oil and gasoline.

She twisted and turned, her nylon collar tightening around her neck as she rolled onto her back. She kicked, ripping her claws across his belly. They were small claws but they caught and held, long enough to make him jump back.

The tiny kitten waited between them, its eyes closed, its lips moving as if the air was its mother's milk. Rusty reached for the kitten and Patsy swung her paw, slapped his face, drawing a thin line of red across his grey nose. Before he could strike back, she turned, leaped over the broken bottle, and shot out of the alley, leaving behind a flash of white tail, a drop of blood, and her blue collar.

Chapter 2

Papa Joe pressed his finger

against a crack in the sidewalk. It wasn't new, he figured, but it might have grown a fraction of an inch or two. He was stepping off the distance from the end of the line to the front door of the Empire when he heard a familiar voice shout, "Good morning, neighbor!"

Over his shoulder, he saw Patsy dart out of the alley and stop in front of the Palace. "Must have felt the quake," Papa Joe said. "That cat can feel all kine things."

Rusty slipped out of the alley and ran in the opposite direction, carrying something in his mouth.

"Sneaky buggah," said Papa Joe.

"Stop that Rusty!" Mr. Goodmorning shouted, hanging out of his third-story window and pointing at the ocean.

Papa Joe pretended not to hear. He did not want to encourage Mr. Goodmorning. The last time the crazy dancer leaned too far out of his window he landed in Hilo Hospital. How he had survived two weeks in that place was a mystery. He cinched his bathrobe, shuffled to the left, and bent down where Mr. Goodmorning could not see him. "Come here," he waved to Patsy. "None of your crazy stuff," he whispered. "Come here."

Patsy stared across the black asphalt.

"That's right," Papa Joe said. "Good to be careful." He checked the street. It was a typical Sunday morning street. Half of Hilo in church, the other half at home sleeping off hangovers. "Come here, girl," he called. "Say hello."

A dog barked.

From around the corner, Mr. Goodmorning shouted, "She has a job to do!"

Patsy sniffed toward the mountain, and Papa Joe thought he knew what she was smelling. He had smelled it too, a hint of vog, a taste of sulfur from the volcano. "How's the boy doing?" he asked, stepping back to his door, waving to his cat friend. "Come over and tell me what's happening in the Palace. You can trust me."

The clouds broke and sunshine poured onto the bumpy asphalt. Patsy marched across the street.

"Come in, come," Papa Joe said, stepping over a pile of soggy newspapers, opening the door to the Empire. "Sit down and I'll fix us a drink."

Mr. Goodmorning shouted, "Don't you get that cat drunk. She's got work to do."

Papa Joe felt Patsy's tail brush against his bare ankle. "Sorry for the mess," he said, locking the door. He hung his bathrobe on the back of his chair. "Haven't had company for a while. I'll only be a minute." From a wicker basket, he took a blue cotton t-shirt and a pair of worn khakis. He made sure the shirt had a pocket, pulled it over his head, and then stepped into the pants. With the shirt tucked in, the pants stayed in place without a belt. "Better?" he asked. "Good enough for your high standards?"

Patsy sat with her back resting against a leather golf bag filled with umbrellas. Some of these had been acquired in trades, others forgotten by customers. Prices ranged from $2 for the retractables that never worked to $15 for the oversized rainbow print that was patched to waterproof perfection with three strips of silver duct tape and had a point on it sharp enough to break a block of ice.

"Pretty girl," Papa Joe said, holding his hand down to Patsy's nose. After she sniffed his fingers, she let him brush the back of his hand along her cheek. "Something missing here." He dug his fingers into her thick fur. "Where's that collar of yours? The one Mimi gave you?"

Patsy stared at him.

Plenty of times, people around town had warned Papa Joe about Patsy's blue eyes. The rumored fact was that strange things happened when Mimi's big cat looked steady and direct at a person. What exactly, depended on who was doing the talking. Teresa at the Mexican restaurant thought

Patsy was capable of hypnotizing people. Doc Trina up at the hospital said something about mind reading. None of it made sense to Papa Joe. To him, a cat was a cat. He stared right back at her slightly crossed blue eyes. "See," he said, remembering the night he had gone swimming with Teresa in the freezing ponds, "You're a cat. That's all."

He remembered the hundred times he had lifted this cat to make specific calculations to determine that she weighed exactly fifteen or sixteen or seventeen pounds. Lots of people thought she was ten pounds heavier, but Papa Joe knew that Patsy's thick fur threw off even the best guessers. Underneath her coat, she was lean and mean, with enough weight to be dangerous but not enough to slow her down, like a UH linebacker or an auntie in charge of a hostess bar.

"Isn't that right?" he said, digging his fingers into her thick fur. "You wouldn't hurt anybody, would you?"

Patsy licked her lips.

"We got to find your collar. You feel that earthquake a minute ago? All kine bad things can happen in earthquakes. First you get an earthquake and then you get a tsunami. If you get washed away in a tsunami without your collar, how are we going to find you?"

He sat down at his desk. "Nasty weather too. First the sun, then the rain. Now some vog. How about a drink?"

While she stepped lightly over a ten-pound sack of coffee, Papa Joe dug a bottle of tequila from the only working drawer in his desk. "Sauza Silver," he said, holding it up for her to see. "Your favorite."

She hopped onto the desk, and Papa Joe poured an inch of tequila into his blue-and-white coffee mug. When she sat down next to a roll of duct tape, he poured her shot into the mug's matching saucer. "Got these from the USS Independence estate sale," he said, savoring the sharp smell of tequila as he pushed the saucer toward her. "Where you off to this Sunday morning?"

Patsy gazed at the saucer.

Papa Joe raised his cup and checked the neon Coors clock on the wall. It had stopped at midnight or noon. "Here's to old friends." He drank the shot and set the empty cup on the table. Patsy sniffed the tequila but did not drink. With clear blue eyes, she looked up at Papa Joe.

He fingered the cup. "Serious this morning, yeah?" He thought long and hard. Poured himself another drink. "Maybe you should go up to the church and say a prayer for her."

Patsy stared at him.

"Don't try no hypnotizing on me."

Patsy's ears shifted right and left.

"No mindreading either." He pointed at his head. "I got nothing in there for you to read. I keep it all subliminal."

Papa Joe checked the clock. Still noon and midnight. "The boy? How's he doing? Still moping around? Getting a movie ready I hope. Haven't seen a movie in a long time."

Carefully, Patsy dipped her paw into the saucer of tequila and licked off a drop.

She could hold her alcohol, Papa Joe knew that. But when she was moody and quiet, like now, she could be a fighter. "Maybe it's better if you stay here where you can't get into trouble." She had been in enough fights. No doubt.

"Now that I think about it, church is no place for a cat like you. Sit around there and hope for someone else to do the job for you. Not your style."

He picked up the morning newspaper, shook it open, and studied the front page. A long time ago he had stopped believing that reading the paper could be of any use except for checking the tide chart, which was mostly right, and the movie schedule, which was mostly wrong. Steamer had made sure of that. He had scheduled and canceled movies so often that Papa Joe had given up counting, and the rest of the people in Hilo had given up coming to the Palace.

"CasaNoir," Papa Joe said, wondering if anyone would ever see it. "At 7:30."

He read the headlines. A bomb had exploded somewhere, a club owner in Honolulu shot, suspects sought, a kid killed in a motorcycle accident.

"The same stuff again." He checked around the edge of the paper and saw that Patsy was still watching him. Poor thing. She was a feeler. After a thing got in her, it wouldn't let go.

He skimmed through the cryptic content of the narrow columns, through print too small for anything good to come from it, and felt his eyes closing. He noticed a headline about oil prices and thought of the five years he had worked on the pipeline in Alaska before waking up with a giant squid headache. He remembered the strong taste of Seattle coffee. Not as good as Dr. Fred's but good enough to cure hangovers.

Carefully, Patsy dipped her paw into the saucer of tequila.

Trying not to think about what had happened to the girl Mimi, Papa Joe struggled to make sense of events in Washington, New York, and Honolulu. The army had raised its maximum age for recruiting, and a guy from Pearl City who had just turned 42 was going to give boot camp a try. He was 5-foot-10 and weighed 240 pounds, had three kids, and would have to run two miles in under 18 minutes to qualify to face the enemy. The newspaper quoted him as saying "I tried to run ten minutes straight yesterday and nearly died."

Under a smaller headline, a young man from Hawaii had died on patrol in Afghanistan. He had been killed two weeks before his scheduled return home. Papa Joe tried but could not pronounce the name of the city where the young man had died.

Papa Joe remembered Mimi knocking lightly on the door. When he opened it, he had seen her face in the moonlight, clean with no lipstick and none of that eye stuff. She had cut her hair short. No more thick ponytail that tossed back and forth when she ran.

She had taken his hand, gripped it hard, and told him that she had a chance to do something important. "Not that life in Hilo isn't important," she said. "Do you understand?"

When she let go of his hand, he said, "Sure, sure, when I was a young man..." and he was about to tell her how as a kid he had run away to join the Marines and seen all kine things he hoped she would never ever see but before he even got to the Marine part, she had thrown her arms around him and squeezed him tight, saying, "I knew you'd understand. Thank you."

Then she had waved to him as she walked off into the moonlight, toward the Pink Church. "Take care of Steamer," she had called. "And the cats! Don't let anything happen to them!"

To get away from his memories, Papa Joe snapped the paper shut and slapped it down on the desk. "Don't you worry," he said to Patsy. "Mimi's a big girl. She can take care of herself. Nothing out there she can't handle."

Papa Joe did not like to lie, even to a cat, but Patsy was his friend, prone to sudden movements, a wanderer, and there was no telling what she would do if she knew the real story. Better for her to stay here. Sit in one place and forget.

"Sit and take it," he said. "You live in the middle of the ocean on one volcano, can't do nothing about what happens out there. You better learn dat."

Patsy jumped to the floor, flicked her tail back and forth, and looked at the door.

"I'm surprised you don't know how to open it." He poured what was left of her tequila into his cup and checked the clock in the belly of the silver-plated elephant above the door. It had stopped running at 4 o'clock. Yesterday? Last week?

While Patsy waited, he drank the last of the tequila. How long could a cat remember one human? He liked her loyalty and dedication but sometimes loyalty and dedication could get a person or cat into trouble. "Cats should know better," he said.

Patsy looked from Papa Joe to the polished doorknob and back again.

"Go find your collar," he said, standing up.

He reached down and dug his fingers through her thick fur, starting at her wide shoulders and pulling back along her ribs. "You be careful," he said. "Lots of bad stuff happening out there."

Unlocking the door, he remembered that he had said the same words to Mimi.

He followed Patsy into the morning light and gave her three good strokes, the way she liked them, from head to tail. "If you go wandering far from home," he said, "you'll get into trouble. Go up to the jail, talk to Manny. He'll tell you."

As she marched uphill, toward the Pink Church, he remembered seeing her go the same way many times with the woman. How long ago? His memory was not as good as it had once been. "I'll look for that collar," he called to her. "Don't bother saying no prayers for me."

He was standing in front of his shop window and anyone passing would have seen him talking to a cat, but he did not care if people saw him. People who did not talk to animals could not be trusted.

Looking down, he saw a thick layer of cat fur stuck to his hands. "Spooky, dat cat." He rubbed his hands together, shook them until cat hair drifted through the air, like confetti. Like memories.

Chapter 3

Ernesto dreamed of flakey white fish in the flickering world of movie light. He stretched his legs, and when they reached over the tattered edges of the violin case, he rolled into the orchestra pit, ran a few steps, and stopped. Awake now, he felt the emptiness in his stomach.

Food, he said to himself. Raw fish and barbeque chicken.

As his eyes adjusted to the shifting shadows, he recognized Steamer sitting in the back row and staring at the screen. Fresh drops of popcorn butter on his t-shirt, an open container of chocolate milk between his legs, and a notepad in hand, he was dug in for a serious session with the flat people.

The man's inability to follow routine disturbed Ernesto. At this time of day Steamer should be prying open a can of tuna, the kind packed in water, and then forking the salty chunks into a clean bowl. Ernesto liked routine. He liked his food in the bowl next to the refrigerator, his water bowl next to the umbrella stand, and he liked to sit in the snack bar with Patsy for breakfast every morning just after the sun came up.

He remembered the white spot on her tail and the tinkling sound of her collar as she ran down the back stairs.

The chase game!

He ran a few steps. Stopped. Felt his hunger growing. How long ago had Patsy interrupted his dream of flakey white fish? Even though Patsy was big and easy to see, she was smart and quick, and there was no point in chasing her if she had a big lead and he had an empty stomach. He thought of the woman slicing off a slab of fresh, red and juicy ahi. He missed her willingness to share and her strong hands capable of wielding sharp kitchen utensils.

Why hadn't she returned with grocery bags full of cat supplies?

He ran a few steps. If Steamer was lost in the world of the flat people that left only Patsy. She would know where to find the woman. He slipped through the curtain, followed the concrete steps to the hole that the woman had cut for him in the wall of the Palace, and ducked through his private door.

Sunlight fell on his alley, his popcorn-machine shelter, and his bed made from old theater seats.

Even from this end of the alley, he could smell his overstuffed dumpster packed with tasty treats. Roasted chicken with just a hint of vog.

But no Patsy.

To hide his disappointment, Ernesto blinked. He had lost her already. The alley was too quiet. No matter where Patsy went dogs barked, cats groaned, and humans fussed. If they weren't bending over to pick her up and call her beautiful, they were pointing at her dark brown mask and chattering about her spooky blue eyes.

Three floors up, Mr. G squeezed out of his window. "Good morning, neighbor," he shouted, waist deep in morning sunshine. "Ernesto, that you down there?"

Ernesto yawned.

"Life is too short for sleeping!"

What did Mr. G mean? Life was meant for sleeping! And eating. That much Ernesto knew from his kitten days, when he had been abandoned without food or water, left to wait in the darkness of a cardboard box, his hunger growing every second. Crying had not helped. Only sleeping had saved him from his growling stomach. No matter what the danger, he yawned, he could escape into a good long nap.

Mr. G leaned his skinny body further out into the air, swinging his arms in a circle that ended with both hands pointed at the street. "She went that way."

Ernesto jumped down to the alley floor, made his way along the wall in the direction Mr. G was pointing. Even if he was wrong, which Mr. G often was, Ernesto did not want to over excite him. Another fall from three stories would not be good, not even for someone as rubbery and hardheaded as Mr. G.

A soft breeze rippled over the dumpster, whistled through the broken seats and swirled in the once mighty popcorn machine. Ernesto remembered it producing endless amounts of tough-to-chew treats before it had popped its last pop and the woman dragged it out here to shelter Ernesto from the rain. From the dumpster, the smell of greasy chicken and dried beer brushed against Ernesto's whiskers. He inhaled deeply, feeling all of life pulse through him on the wings of stinky leftovers.

Was that Monterey Jack?

"There. Behind the dumpster," Mr. G called. "That's where I seen her. Something strange going on. That girl Patsy with the white spot on her tail is into some kine trouble. There, behind the dumpster. I seen one kidnapping!"

Ernesto had important things to do. What, he was not certain, but he had come here to do something. He checked behind the dumpster and found an empty food bowl and Angelica feeding an endless line of kittens. Too many mouths to feed. He counted them, one through six. Where had they come from? Ernesto dug deep into his mind but found no answers. He watched them eat. However they had managed it, they were lucky to have found Angelica. She had a small appetite and enjoyed sharing. Not like her friend Rusty. He could eat platefuls without breathing and without a thought to those less fortunate.

Ernesto looked up as a puff of thick white fur drifted by his whiskers, leaving behind the powerful scent of night-blooming jasmine. It mixed magically with the sweet smell of Angelica the Calico's milk, and Ernesto felt the world warming around him, becoming soft and cozy with memories. He was cast ashore on a warm blanket next to a misty kitchen sink, where he blinked at Mimi who was dipping chicken thighs into a pool of warm butter. He closed his eyes and dreamed of the day when the woman would return. She would hold him in her arms and they would be the best of friends, and later he would show her Angelica and her kittens so she could fill their bowl with Scientific Diet, a type of hardtack not much for taste but good for filling a void and making small bodies strong.

"Wake up!"

Ernesto did not know how long he had been sleeping but the sun felt like a warm blanket. When he stretched, his front paw touched something sticky, a tiny red spot that smelled of cheese and chicken and blood.

"One of the babies is missing," Mr. G shouted down from his window. "Rusty took it. Patsy ran across the road to the Empire. The wrong direction."

Ernesto followed a trail of Patsy fur to the sidewalk. He stopped at the street. He did not mind the sidewalk but he did not like the street. It led away from the Palace. A cat had to be careful when crossing the street. Patsy did it all the time, but he was not Patsy, who knew the secrets of crossing over to the Empire.

"There," Mr. G called. "See? Pick it up."

In the gutter, Patsy's collar sparkled. From the day the woman had given it to her, Patsy had worn this collar. No matter how frayed or dirty it had become, before today she had never taken it off, not even when hunting. If she needed a moving treat, she'd flick the metal tag behind her head, burying it deep in her thick fur so she could stalk her prey silently.

With his tongue and four fangs, Ernesto managed to pick up the collar.

"Go up the road," Mr. G called. "I seen Patsy go that way while you were sleeping. Up toward the church." He pointed at the ocean. "Or go that way. A kitten is missing."

Ernesto looked both ways. He did not like to leave the Palace. He had never left the Palace. Should he go left or right? He decided to retrace his steps back into the alley and blinked goodbye to Mr. G. It might be a long journey and he had not yet eaten breakfast.

"That's right!" Mr. G shouted. "Go get help! No one expects you to save the world by yourself."

Holding the collar with his sharp teeth, Ernesto squeezed through the hole that Mimi had cut for him. Remembering the tip of Patsy's tail waving white, he ran up the stairs. He stopped for a moment as he remembered Mimi's fingers prying open a can of salty tuna. Where was she? Did Mr. G say she had been kidnapped?

He stepped between the heavy black curtains and stopped at the edge of the stage to let his eyes adjust to the shifting mixture of flickering light and darkness.

The man was still sitting in the back row. Why wasn't he handing the woman a strong cup of coffee, touching her lightly with his lips so that she would sit up in bed and realize it was time for the wrestling game?

Ernesto jumped down from the stage, slipped under the seats, and found an orange tentacle next to a coke stain. He sniffed the dried cuttlefish. Spicy! And stiff! But some treats grew better with age. Dried cuttlefish was one of them. He snapped up the rubbery treat and swallowed it without chewing. Only Papa Joe's friend Manny could bite through cuttlefish that old.

Crawling under seats, he found a lonely kernel of popcorn, a carton of chocolate milk, and the man's rubber slippers. He licked a tiny molecule of butter from the petals of the lonely kernel, then snapped up its skeleton. Standing over the chocolate milk, he dipped his tongue deep into the container but could not reach the sweet liquid. While he was thinking of tipping it over and drinking from the spill, the meager calories provided by the cuttlefish and popcorn produced a rush of mind activity and cat morality. The man was his best friend and he did not want to steal from him, even if it was food, which technically belonged to everyone on a first-come first-served basis. But the floor angled downward and if he spilled the milk, he would not be able to catch or drink all of it. Waste not, want not was a good rule.

On the screen, a flat man and a flat woman sat at a table covered with flat food. Two huge bowls of white rice overlooked a valley of spicy chicken, a river of slippery flat noodles, a jungle of kim chee. Ernesto sniffed hard, but as usual the flat food had no smell. Even the kim chee with its robust red and deadly orange petals carried no scent. In the flat world, even this strongest and most feared cabbage was only a shadow of its real self. Half cabbage, half light. Odorless.

Feeling his hunger growing, Ernesto raised his tail in the air, turned his back on Steamer, and headed for the lobby. He followed the old carpet down the stairs, checked the snack bar and behind the refrigerator, usually good places to find a stray snack but today there were none, only dust. He searched under the couch, in the office, the ticket booth, the closet, the bathroom with the extra-large drinking bowls, and when he found nothing, he ran back up the stairs to the man and his chocolate milk.

The man looked down at him and said, "What are we going to do?"

Ernesto did not know. He could not concentrate. No woman, no food. He thought of empty spaces in his mind, in his stomach, in his world. He wondered why Patsy had driven away all the mice?

"I can't live without her," the man said.

Ernesto licked his lips.

Why didn't the man tire of sitting and go find the woman? She had an endless supply of energy and could play wrestling games all through the night. If he asked her, she would go to the snack bar, to the green refrigerator capable of hiding immense supplies of food, and in its silent coolness she would find slices of bread and cheese, bowls of strawberries and cream, tubs of chocolate ice cream. She would bring these treats to the man to give him energy and strength. They would eat. Then they would play the chase game and wrestle. Then they would sleep, and Ernesto would eat leftovers for them.

Steamer looked at him. "Where's Patsy?"

Ernesto blinked.

"We have to keep an eye on her."

Ernesto remembered the tip of her white tail flashing.

"She's our only girl now."

Ernesto remembered the collar in his mouth. He saw the flat people on the big screen. The woman was walking away from the man, up the stairs to a plane. She turned and waved. A whale appeared.

Ernesto felt the world turning underneath him. Where were Mimi, Patsy and her collar? Too many things were missing.

lz

Chapter 4

S teamer watched the screen.

Turning his back to the rolling credits and crossing the sagging floor, he felt as if he were almost alive. He could walk. He could wave his hands over his head. He could shout into the rafters. "Hello! Anybody up there?"

He inhaled moldy air and memories.

"No," he said. "Nobody up there."

He glanced back at names moving too fast to be read. All of them had been dead for years, but a moment ago he had seen them walking across the screen.

"Don't think crazy," he said, heading for the projection booth. "And don't talk to yourself. You have a job to do. Get ready for the trustees so you can pay the rent. First things first."

He walked straight to the projector, flicked the power switch off, and watched the screen go black, the lights go up. "Do you promise to stop talking to yourself? I promise."

His let his legs carry him to the coat rack that Papa Joe had found at the USS Independence estate sale. The door hidden behind it was open wide enough for a cat to slip through. "Patsy, you in there?"

His hand touched the brass doorknob. It felt real. Solid. His brain must be working. Thoughts were in there warming up. He held his breath, pushed open the door, and stepped into the morning light.

The table was still in the middle of the room. The message from Mimi still on Bogart's face. He touched the chair, the dresser, and the queen-size bed. Everything was still in place. Now he could breathe. He tucked the sheets in, spread the blanket over the pillows. Someday soon he'd go over to Papa Joe's Empire and buy a cot, an army cot just like Joe's, and then he'd give this bed to someone who needed it. He did not want to sleep in it. He wanted a cot made for one.

Sunlight poured through the line of windows, revealing a high ceiling that was not a ceiling, just redwood rafters and the underside of the Palace's tin roof. "Anybody up there?" Steamer called.

He twisted at the waist, jumped up and down, did one jumping jack. "Have to stay fit," he said, grabbing the drapes and shaking them. Cat hair and dust drifted through the air. "What's this?" From the windowsill he picked up his video camera and a plastic baggie. The baggie had a tiny note inside, written in blue ink: *Eat Me First!* How long had these cookies been hiding here?

He set the camera on the table and opened the bag. When he held it to his nose and inhaled, he recognized the sweet scent of Oreo cookies. Jumbo size. Three of them. "Perfect, creamy and chocolate. That's what Ernesto would say." He broke off a piece of cookie. In the rainforest called Hilo, the cookie had managed to stay crisp. Could probably stay fresh for a hundred years more if Ernesto didn't find it.

For a moment he stood still, feeling the warm sun on his shoulder. "Waste not, want not. That's what Mimi would say." He dropped the cookie in the bag and sealed it. He had things to do. He would make a list. Accomplish stuff.

He sat down at the table and brushed cat hair off Bogart's chin. Patsy had been here. She was everywhere. He picked up the blue pen and flipped the poster onto its blank side. He didn't want to throw it away. He didn't want to keep it.

As he pressed the pen to paper, he thought of her. The more he thought, the more the pen wanted to race across the poster's slick surface. He scribbled a few circles and drew a stick woman with a huge heart. When the ink smell made his head spin, he told himself that he was becoming too much like the cats, smelling everything. Holding his breath, he forced the pen to make a list.

1. *Keep an eye on Papa Joe, don't let him drink (too much).*
2. *Feed the Bopper.*
3. *Keep Mr. Goodmorning from leaning out the window.*
4. *Visit Manny in jail.*
5. *Finish the woodwork in the orchestra pit.*
6. *Stop talking to yourself.*
7. *Finish the movie cuts. Make it positive and uplifting. That's what people need these days. Come up with a new title. Fatal Desire? Add some stuff from old karate movies that will keep the action junkies happy and give the trustees the subtitles they want.*
8. *Clean up the snack bar.*
9. *Fix the toilet.*

He needed one more point. All good lists had ten points. He looked around for Ernesto, a good source of inspiration in these matters. Ernesto was a good friend, somewhat limited when it came to conversation but always around when needed. He never wandered, unlike his namesake who had gone off to an ungrateful Bolivia. Unlike Patsy, who wandered all over Hilo.

10. *Write a letter to Mimi*

He moved the pen across the paper, knowing that she would not forget, knowing that she could never leave.

Dearest Mimi,
You have been gone so long. I'm sitting in our room thinking only of you. Silence fills each moment with thoughts of love and longing. Remember how we used to swim together in the freezing ponds? We'll be together soon and we'll hold each other in the moonlight.

He crossed out the paragraph, crossed out the crossings, and found a blank spot.

Dear Mimi,
The cats are fine. No problems here. Saw in the paper that tuna is on sale. 12 cans for $6. You never got that kine deal! It's Safeway tuna but Ernie eats it (is there anything he won't eat?).
It's Sunday morning and I'm getting ready for the trustees to visit. Making a list of things to do. I've got an idea for a movie blend that I think will blow them away. Instead of showing one movie, I'm going to jam three or four together. Like a remix of an old song. Good stuff.
Papa Joe says hello. He's the usual, chasing away customers and coming by everyday to ask when I'll show a new movie.
I wish you were here.
Patsy and Ernie are fine. We'll take care of things. Ernie has grown fond of

sleeping in the orchestra pit, in that old violin case. Patsy has moved off the bed and sleeps in the projection room, in the file cabinet. Ernie was sitting with me just a moment ago. Patsy is around here somewhere. You know her, probably sleeping or exploring. Looking for secret spots, new horizons.

I'm eating right and keeping up with the paper work: electricity bill, property tax, cable bill, phone bill, water bill, rubbish bill, film rental, grant applications.

Attendance has been good and we have no money problem. Today I'm going to work on the orchestra pit and replace the two rotted planks under the string section.

Steamer studied his letter. There was only a little room at the bottom of the page, but he did not want to stop. While writing he had felt close to her. Should he tell her about the earthquake? The feel of a storm in the air? No. He wanted to tell her good things, only good things.

Angelica the Calico had her kittens. Yesterday she showed up with seven of them and now they're all out there in the alley. I thought of you and left out a bowl of food and water. Will refill them today. Every time I look at the horizon, I think of you and how proud I am of you and your desire to make things right. Please don't

forget me, Ernesto and Patsy. We're
waiting for you. Working and waiting for
the day when we will be with you.
Everything here is fine.
Love always,

He stopped writing and stood up, brushed strands of Patsy's fur off his hands. When the light from the windows touched him, he took a deep breath and forced himself to forget.

"Get to work!" he said. "Now!"

He picked up the camcorder. She had given it to him as a New Year's present. It was not the newest model but it took decent footage and was indestructible. To prove it, she had tossed it from the roof.

Looking up three stories, he had seen it coming, a camera dropping through a sky filled with rain and fireworks, and he had caught it, juggled it, and pressed the power switch. Like a professional, he had turned and caught Papa Joe lighting a string of firecrackers, filmed explosions climbing up the Palace marquee while a Chinese dragon danced in the streets.

Telling himself to forget, he unlatched the window, leaned out, and aimed the camera at the harbor. No one should die far from home. He wanted her to see the breeze rippling over the water and the narrow street that led from the ocean to the mountain. He filmed a black car moving slowly up the black asphalt, past the empty storefronts, past the Empire, up the mountain, toward the Pink Church.

A dog barked.

The Mailbox Bopper rounded the corner, swinging his bat, heading for the Palace. "Crap," Steamer said but kept filming. The Bopper was one of her people. "One of Mimi's projects. And now he's my project. He's on the official list." The Bopper would have to be broken of his mailbox habit. Zooming in, Steamer tried to find the Bopper's face in the shadows of his hooded sweatshirt.

After stopping in front of the two mailboxes attached to the wall of Blister's New Age Gym, the Bopper cocked his aluminum bat over his shoulder. He stepped closer, pressed his bare feet into solid concrete.

A dog barked.

"Hey," Steamer yelled. "No more bopping."

The Bopper stopped in mid-swing and looked up, his eyes hidden behind dark glasses. "Who says?"

"I say. Me. Steamer."

"So what?"

"Mimi told me to tell you."

"You're not Mimi."

"She's watching you."

"Where?" With a quick flick of his wrists, he swung the bat, crashing it into the mailboxes. As the smashing sound echoed through the air, he shook off his hood and tramped toward the Palace with his bat raised.

"I did it," he shouted. "I'll do it again."

Steamer was pulling himself inside when he saw a woman and boy turn the corner at the ocean-end of the street. They were headed up the mountain but on the safe side of the street. If they were from

Hilo, they would know enough to stay there, clear of the Bopper. Filmed through the telephoto lens, they looked like they were dressed for church. The woman in a white blouse, black slacks, and black high heels. The boy in a stiff white shirt, pressed blue jeans and black high-top sneakers. But if they were headed for church, why was she carrying an army duffel bag?

"Stay on the other side of the street," Steamer whispered.

The woman looked at the address above the surf shop, checked it against a piece of paper in her hand, shook her head, and crossed the street.

The Bopper shouted up at him, "You say hello to Mimi for me!" He pointed the aluminum bat at the Palace's neon sign. "You tell Mimi to come back!"

"She isn't going to like what you did to that mailbox."

"You tell her I seen her cat that girl with the mask headed up to the church."

The woman checked the address of Mr. Goodmorning's place. Then she turned and crossed the street again, her boy in tow, sharing a music player, wires leading from her hip to both their heads, one ear bud apiece. She stopped in front of the Empire.

"I seen her go into Joe's place," the Bopper yelled, turning to point at the Empire.

The woman tapped twice on the Empire's window as the Bopper stepped into the street, giving her a long look.

Still filming, Steamer thought about yelling down to the woman that Papa Joe didn't open the door for anyone on Sunday morning except maybe Mimi, and Mimi wasn't here, so she should run like hell. Steamer felt something rub against his leg. He looked down and saw Ernesto holding Patsy's collar in his mouth.

"Now we got problems," Steamer said.

He felt the frayed blue nylon and remembered Mimi cutting the end, burning the ragged edge with a candle, and then waiting for it to cool so she could test the length. He thought about her hands for a long time, and when he looked back out the window, the street was empty. A soft breeze blew through the telephone wires. Steamer put down the camera and picked up the pen, wrote on his official list:

   10.   *Find Patsy.*

He took the nylon collar from Ernesto and remembered holding Mimi, being in her arms, touching her lips, tasting her desire, and he felt her inside him as he drifted across the endless distance that divided them.

Chapter 5

P atsy followed memories of the woman through gasoline fumes, burger smoke, and a vapor cloud of Mrs. Tokunaga's sweet red roses. Still going uphill, she passed a pawnshop, two small churches, and a massage parlor that offered tarot readings.

She stopped to play hide-and-seek with the children at the YWCA. Pretending to be incapable of making sharp turns or climbing tall trees, she chose the most obvious hiding place, under the swings, and let the screeching girls catch and hold her so she could feel their tiny hands in her fur.

Happy and looking for more excitement, she chased a gecko all the way to the museum, cornered it at the entrance to the Plantation Days exhibit, and tapped it gently to see its own death. Only the tiny beating of its heart betrayed its acting skills. As a black car passed slowly going downhill, disappearing toward the ocean, she moved her paw, letting her green and yellow prisoner escape. The gecko, its tail still attached, pressed itself flat and squiggled to safety under the museum door.

Impressed with its effort and skills, Patsy crossed the street intending to say hello to the black Persian who lived behind the senior citizen retirement center. She looked everywhere but could not find him. Sitting next to his empty basket lined with Banyan tree shadows, she remembered Mimi picking him up and holding him close to her chest, using her fingers to comb out clumps of long black hair. She crossed the parking lot and walked directly uphill, following the sidewalk, paying no attention to the gang of sharp-beaked birds that watched her suspiciously from the mango tree.

When she reached the Pink Church, the doors were closed. In the parking lot, rows of tired trucks and sleeping cars, most of them clean, some even shiny, waited for their owners. Patsy said hello to the ones she knew best. Mr. Fukunaga's pickup. Ms. Betty's silver VW Bug. The battered jeep owned by the bartender at the *Second To Last Call.*

She stopped at the concrete steps that led to the main entrance. The two wide doors with brass handles made her think of Mimi's strength and her ability to break through all doors, even these two monsters. Now that the woman had disappeared it was Patsy's duty to find a way through them, to find the courage to face the dying man and ask him if he had any clues that would aid in the search for Mimi.

This would not be easy.

"Not me," Steamer always said when Mimi pointed up the road at the Pink Church and asked if he was going. "That stuff scares me. Something wrong about keeping a guy nailed to a cross."

Like Steamer, Patsy did not enjoy looking at the man on the cross, and she did not understand how Mimi could kneel for hours gazing at his suffering, but on the night of her disappearance, she had displayed all the signs of an impending trip to the Pink Church. She had left food on her plate, smoked a cigarette behind the Palace, and paced back and forth in the alley, like a restless cat. Then she was gone. Maybe she was inside now, dipping her fingers into the water bowl that Patsy found perfect for drinking. Or lighting candles. Or dropping coins in the collection box.

Patsy hopped to the top of a pickup truck. Through stained-glass windows, she saw people kneeling and standing and kneeling again, like Ernesto waking from a nap, sitting up and lying down, going back to sleep because he had forgotten why he had woken up.

She thought of the woman kneeling with her hands folded and her head bowed, whispering to the man on the cross, "I love you. Forgive me. I love you."

Patsy opened her mouth to say the magic words. And then the miracle happened. Bells rang,

45

doors swung open, and people poured out of the church, smiling, looking up at the sky, and saying, "Thank god!"

"A beautiful day!"

"A long one!"

A small boy shielded his eyes from the sun and said, "Mommy, it's going to rain."

At the top of the steps, a tall man in a black robe greeted people as they poured out of the church. He shook their hands, kissed a baby on the cheek, kissed another on the head. Waved goodbye.

Pasty remembered Angelica's kitten and thought again about their mysterious origins. Did humans come here to collect their babies? Patsy had never seen it happen but perhaps the distribution took place inside, somewhere in a secret room. But if so, why had Mimi never collected one for the Palace?

"Jesus loves the children!" she heard a woman say, brushing sweat off her forehead as she chased a small girl across the parking lot.

Too quick for the black robe to notice, Patsy slipped off the truck, up the stairs and into the church. While she waited under a pew for an old couple without children to leave, she thought that of all the churches she had visited with Mimi, the Pink Church was her favorite. She liked its high ceiling and the way the sun passed through the colored windows, covering all the statues in a multi-colored glow. Today the air tasted of perfume and incense. The man in black must have been swinging the golden globe again, spreading the sweet smelling smoke through the church, sending it upward to the faraway ceiling.

When the man in black returned, he motioned for the old couple to follow him. They disappeared through three doors. In the red and gold window above them, a winged creature carried a smiling baby into the clouds. Maybe the old couple was behind the doors asking for a small human or a kitten. Mimi always chose the door on the left or right but she never came out with a baby.

Usually, she stopped to kneel below the man on the cross. The last time she had been here she had looked up at him and talked for a long time, telling him that saying a rosary was a lot of work for small sins, and she didn't even know if she had a rosary. Maybe she could borrow one, but if she did, and if anything happened to her, she should get to go up there.

Patsy did not know if she liked rosaries or sins or praying, or going up there if it meant being with the suffering man. But she liked little rooms, especially little dark rooms that smelled of church smoke. Maybe Mimi was in there now, or maybe the man in black could tell her the way to get up there. She waited until the old couple left, still without children, then made her way under the pews and stopped in front of the three doors.

The winged creature was still carrying the baby into the sky.

Patsy waited for the woman to appear. The doors did not open. If it would bring the woman back, Patsy would commit all the necessary sins. She did not know the exact procedure for sinning, but she knew it had something to do with drinking tequila, smoking cigarettes in the alley, and saying stuff about the man nailed to the cross.

Patsy confessed to the winged creature that she was sorry for drinking tequila with Papa Joe. She waited. When nothing happened, she said she was sorry for all the times she had nibbled tuna from Ernie's bowl.

When the woman still did not appear and the doors did not open, Patsy followed the granite path to the altar where she had seen Mimi kneel to wait for a tiny snack, a flat piece of white bread, not even a mouthful. She could not kneel so Patsy sat with her eyes focused on the man hanging from the cross. Patsy did not understand why people folded their hands and looked so lovingly at the small bits of food provided by the cross man and his friend in the black robe. Not even Ernie would get excited about a snack so small.

Gazing up at the man above the altar, Patsy tried to say the magic words. She tried again but still the woman did not appear. Did she have to actually say the words for him to hear her prayer?

Perhaps the man on the cross was too tired to perform a miracle today. He looked exhausted. She felt a great emptiness inside her and asked for a smaller miracle. Could the man at least return her blue collar? I love you, she tried to say, but her collar did not appear.

Disappointed, Patsy followed the woman's regular path out the back door and up the hill, along the side street known for its skinny cats and banana trees. She passed old houses made of wood, a bathtub in a yard, an outrigger canoe in a garage.

After turning right then left, she shot across an empty lot, avoiding a hole in the fence that led to the grammar school and chose instead a narrow path through a bamboo forest that was tall and cool and filled with tiny green birds smart enough to stay up high.

From the edge of the bamboo, she watched the front of the jail. She waited until the guard at the door went inside, then she crossed the street and hurried along the chain-link fence. There was no point in trying the front door. Unlike the men in black at the Pink Church, the men in black at the jail kept all the doors locked. Even when Mimi arrived with a backpack stuffed with snacks and books, colorful books with glossy pictures of waterfalls and green valleys, they allowed her inside only for a short time, and only after much head shaking and arm waving.

Patsy ran to the back of the jail, where Mimi kept a food bowl for the cats who called the jail their home. Patsy's favorite was an old Siamese female who had once been a fast runner and explorer of the Big Island. A very curious cat, the Siamese had found a way under the chain-link fence and chosen the jail for her retirement. She liked the way the humans inside never ran and rarely made quick or unexpected movements. Most of them, even the young ones, preferred to spend their time lying in bed, in small rooms, only occasionally jumping up to slam their fists against solid walls. In exchange for these minor disturbances, the old Siamese could rest her legs in a safe place far from the Hilo rain.

Patsy looked for her among the men trapped in the narrow space formed by four walls of chain-link fence. In their orange jump suits and black rubber slippers, they paced back and forth, stopping only to look up at the swirls of barbed wire at the top of the fence.

Were these men like the prisoners at the Palace?

The flats were dangerous men crowded into tiny cells. They'd punch each other and growl like dogs at the world outside. Sometimes they'd escape by shooting everyone in sight or crawling through damp tunnels. Then they'd drink whiskey, grab women, and try to kiss them. But they were not good at the chase game, and the flat guards always caught them by chasing them with sirens and shouting at them through bullhorns. When the prisoners could no longer stand the noise, they'd throw their arms in the air, and the guards would strap them into chairs that made the lights flicker.

Patsy turned away from the men and checked the food bowl. It was empty except for red ants crawling over its sticky surface. She pressed her nose against the ground, and deep in the greenness of it she thought she smelled the woman.

The fence shook, and she jumped back. A man with wide shoulders and rough hands stood on the other side, looking down at her.

"Come here, girl," he said, squatting down. He pressed his thick fingers through the chain link. "Come here."

Patsy stepped closer to the fence. She pressed her nose against the rusting metal. Rough and cold, it reminded her of the animal shelter, her first home.

"Pretty girl."

Patsy brushed against the fence, but the man's hands could not reach her. His fingers dug at the empty space between the double layers of chain link. He looked at her with dark eyes, and she wondered if he knew what had happened to Mimi. Had he seen her books, their pictures of waterfalls and white beaches? Had the Siamese told him about her slow walks on the misty trails in Waipio Valley? Or the taste of coppery rainwater in Volcano?

Love, she tried to say. Love

A tear formed at the corner of the man's eye.

Behind him, the other prisoners paced back and forth, back and forth.

Chapter 6

Papa Joe lifted the Virgin

Mary by her elbows. "Five pounds," he said, about to turn her upside down. Then a woman tapped on his window.

"You be quiet," he whispered to the statue, setting her next to King Kamehameha in the window display. "This is none of your business." He positioned the golden Madonna so that the king's outstretched hand touched her shoulder. "Just sit there and be a nice couple."

The woman tapped again, a gentle tap that shook the wire hanging from her ear. How long had she been standing there?

Papa Joe scratched the three days of whiskers on his chin, wondering if Patsy had anything to do with his lack of focus. A cat capable of spreading memories was certainly capable of creating other mischief.

The woman pointed at the door, and Papa Joe noticed that the wire hanging from her ear reached her shoulder and disappeared behind her back. "These days most people have at least one or two wires sticking out of them," he told the Madonna as he walked to the door. His friend Manny had relayed this fact to him during a tequila-inspired lecture about a future when people would wear Teflon implants under their skin so they could stop carrying credit cards and listen to AM radio in the bathtub.

As he opened the door, he saw the Bopper run into the alley.

"Excuse me," the woman said. "I am looking for the Empire."

She had a gentle voice and a clean face. Papa Joe liked that, but the small gold cross hanging from her neck worried him. He wondered if it had anything to do with the wire attached to her ear.

"I am looking for a man called Papa Joe."

An Army duffel bag rested at her feet. Papa Joe thought that any woman who carried a duffel bag instead of a suitcase could not be all bad. "I figure you weigh a hundred pounds," he said. "Maybe ninety."

"I am not certain."

"You can be certain," he said. "You're either a hundred or ninety. Maybe somewhere in between."

He checked the street and saw a black SUV turn the corner from the ocean. "Come in, come," he said motioning her inside.

When he reached to help her with the duffel bag, she pulled it back, lifted it onto her shoulder and said, "It is not heavy."

"You're strong for one ninety pounder. That bag must weigh fifty, sixty pounds."

"I can carry it."

As she passed him, he smelled ivory soap and noticed that the wire led to a small boy moving quickly and easily behind her, keeping pace so that the wire never lost its slack. "Sit there," Papa Joe said, pointing at a leather armchair.

He closed the door, bolted it shut. When he turned around, he saw her kiss the boy on the forehead.

Papa Joe was not good at guessing the age of children. The boy was small, he knew that. Maybe only forty pounds. Smaller than the duffel bag. "You get one big boy there," he said, sitting down behind the desk. "What he weigh? Sixty, seventy pounds?" Despite his name, Papa Joe had little experience with children and he did not want to offend the boy.

"I have something for you," the woman said, digging into her duffel bag. The air was thick with the smell of books and a little kid and a soapy young woman.

"I got plenty duffel bags," Papa Joe said.

The woman set a shoebox on the desk. Duct-taped to the top of the box was a thick envelope. "Johnny," she said, "wanted me to give this to you."

"Johnny?"

"He said you were his uncle." She gave the boy her earphone, brushed a clump of cat hair off the chair, and sat down. The boy moved in front of her, his hands on her knees and his eyes on Papa Joe.

"Tall and thin? Always working?" Papa Joe asked. "Good fisherman? Got this scar on his cheek?"

"He did not say he was a fisherman."

"His father one good fisherman. Could tell the weather by smell."

"He did not speak of his father."

Papa Joe looked at the box, shook it. He guessed that it weighed a couple of pounds. He felt the sticky edges of the tape. His name and address were written in deep blue ink, in ragged letters that stretched across the entire envelope. "He likes to travel, that boy. Like me when I was younger."

"He said you were a good man."

Papa Joe looked at the bottle of tequila on his desk and felt thirsty. He thought he was a good man, except for a few things. No one is perfect. He picked up the bottle, tightened the cap, and placed it carefully in the drawer. He did not think it was correct to offer a drink to a mother and her son this early in the morning. "Patsy," he said, "the girl cat from next door came by earlier and got me started. Nice cat but moody, kinda spooky eyes. Heavy drinker."

The woman fingered her cross.

"Don't get her wrong," Papa Joe said, picking up a dive knife that he had acquired from Manny in a trade for a five-pound bag of Dr. Fred's Special Blend, the only coffee with enough caffeine to keep

Manny awake on the graveyard shift. "Patsy has values." He slit the duct tape, peeled the envelope away from the box.

"She goes to church. Think she's up there right now. She wouldn't be drinking this early, normally, except I can't blame her. We've had some problems around here." He sliced the envelope open and pulled out a thick wad of notebook paper. It felt heavy and warm. He recognized the paper from when he was a kid at St. Joe's, the spiral notebook kine with three holes, black lines, and frayed edges.

> *Hey Joe,*
>
> *It's been a long time. I can't remember the last time we talked or wrote. I got a favor to ask, and I'm sitting here at 2 in the morning, figuring how to ask it. I know what kind of guy you are so I know you can't turn me down, not when it comes to something like this. I made a mistake. Maybe more than one. So be it. A guy's got to make a living, and get a start. And sometimes a guy makes a mistake.*

As he shuffled through the pages, counting but not reading, Papa Joe wished he had another sip of tequila. "One long letter," he said. When deciding whether to buy used books, Papa Joe never bothered to read much, only the first and last pages. He liked quick starts and happy endings in books that smelled good. This letter smelled like coffee, air-conditioning, and Ivory soap. Not a bad reading smell.

"Five pages," he said, as he peeked at the last paragraph of the last page.

> *Anyway, that's what I did. Please take care of them. Antonia has been good to me. The boy too. Like I said, he's a smart kid. These two are all I have in this world. I'll be back for them as soon as I can. You know how these things are. The shoebox is for you, to help. She wanted you to have it. I'm sure you'll put it to good use.*
>
> > *Take care of them, please,*
> > *Johnny.*

Papa Joe looked at the boy, trying to see Johnny in him. "Your name is Antonia?"

"Yes," the woman said, wrapping her arm around the boy and pulling him closer. "And this is Anthony."

"Two good names."

Papa Joe put the letter down and stood up. He walked around the desk and took the woman's hand, shook it, then did the same with the boy, with the same strength, as a sign of respect. Then he grabbed him under the arms and picked him up, asking, "How much you weigh?"

The boy's feet dangled in the air but he did not squirm. That was a good sign. He was a brave boy, and Papa Joe felt life in him and saw how the woman's hands tightened on the chair.

"He's clean," Papa Joe said. "Quick, I bet. A good eater."

"He is a healthy boy," she said.

"Steady now," Papa Joe said. He told himself that he could lift many things bigger than this boy. He could lift stacks of books and cardboard boxes filled with cans of tuna. He could lift a fifty-pound bag of coffee. He tossed the boy into the air and caught him. "Forty-five pounds. That's what I say."

The boy said, "Forty-five pounds."

"That's right. Good."

The woman watched Papa Joe closely, the cross bright around her neck.

"No need to worry," Papa Joe said to her. He was a stiff old man, especially in the mornings before a good drink, but he was still strong and he understood the importance of keeping a boy safe. A boy needed to face the world in one piece. "I figure if I can lift a boy I can keep an eye on him."

He sat the boy down on the desk so that he was facing his mother.

"Too bad Patsy isn't here," Papa Joe said. He wanted to remember the old days and how his father cared for him, but that was a long time ago and he had no memories of that time. He guessed that the boy and his mother would be easy to care for because they were like cats. Quiet and strong and always watching. And the woman had a collar, like Patsy.

"I'm sure she'd like to meet you."

The boy sat with his legs hanging off the desk, his small hands rubbing the polished hard wood. He picked up a wispy clump of cat hair and handed it to Papa Joe.

"You got good eyes, Anthony." He rubbed the cat hair between his fingers, then stuck it in his shirt pocket. "You got to be careful. All kine cats live around here," he said, turning to the boy's mother. "Ernesto stays at the Palace. And there's Angelica who's always getting pregnant. And then there's Patsy, Ernesto's sister. Sturdy gal wears a mask and has a white spot on her tail. Moody, small claws. Leaves her fur everywhere."

He didn't tell the woman that she had eyes like Patsy. Instead, he took the tequila from the drawer and poured himself a shot, to help with all the talking he had to do. "Johnny says it's my job to take care of you." The first sip made him feel as if he had just brushed his teeth. The second made him see Johnny holding the boy and his mother. "He's a good boy. Helped around here whenever he could. Did things. I owe him." He remembered the letter, folded it, and stuffed it in his shirt pocket. "Don't get me wrong. Drinking is not good for small boys and cats."

The boy nodded.

"When Patsy starts drinking she can get into all kines trouble, especially around here. Lots of places for trouble."

The three of them looked at the inside of the Empire. It was a small shop, piled high with boxes and books. Stacks of coffee bags and old magazines littered the floor. Shelves lined with statues and flowerpots covered one wall. A surfboard hung from the ceiling. In the corner, a bike with fat tires was parked in a claw-foot tub. On the wall above the side door, tulip-shaped lights cast dusty light into even dustier shadows.

"Lots of stuff," Papa Joe said, remembering how he had acquired each piece.

"Nice things," Antonia said.

"Not very homey," said Papa Joe. He finished his drink and sat back, resting his feet on a five-pound bag of coffee. He was thinking that his sleeping area in the attic was too small for them. He had an army cot near the air vents, a card table, a footlocker and a canvas director's chair. If he wanted to read, he could open the vents to let in moonlight and the green-and-yellow glow from the Palace's neon sign. That was good enough for him but not good enough for a boy and his mother.

"Kinda crowded here," Papa Joe said, turning and looking out the window. He poured another shot of tequila into his cup. Sipped. Waited for insights. Slowly, a thick cloud of inspiration formed in his head. "You can't stay here," he said.

The boy stopped smiling and looked at the floor. The woman said, "I understand."

"But," Papa Joe said, looking across the street. "Do you like movies?"

Chapter 7

E rnesto followed Steamer out of the bedroom, watching him jam Patsy's collar into his pocket. They were on the move! Then the man paused to touch the projector, look up at the ceiling while Ernesto waited at the door to the balcony. Before Ernesto could stop him, the man was attached to his computer.

"Just for a couple seconds or two," Steamer said, touching buttons, sipping cold coffee, coffee that Ernesto had tried two days ago and even then found too bitter for drinking. "I've got an idea. I want to see how it looks on the big screen. "

Hoping the man would follow him, Ernesto brushed against his leg, hooked his tail around his ankle and walked to the door.

"We'll find her. Don't worry," Steamer said. "Give me a few seconds to work on tonight's movie. I know I have those files here somewhere."

Ernesto sat in the back row of the balcony, in Patsy's favorite seat, and kept an eye on him. Once the man was attached to his computer, there was no telling how long he would stay there held prisoner by the knobs, keys, and tasteless plastic mouse.

Now that the woman was not here to wrestle Steamer away from the computer, Ernesto was certain that the man was spending too many hours playing with the flat people. Everyday, Steamer watched them closely on the tiny screen, making them walk backward then rush forward, retracing their steps while he begged them to do it right so he could get them in the movie. Then he would sit in the balcony and watch them on the big screen. Any day now Ernesto expected him to start acting like one of them. Any second, just like them, he would break out in song or march off on stiff legs wrapped in shiny black boots, jabbing his fist in the air.

Ernesto wanted to warn Steamer to run for his life, to go outside where the flat people could not reach him. But he was a cat and could not find the words. He wanted to say that despite the good things they did some of the time, the flat people were nasty and mean and repetitive. They shot each other dead then celebrated by dancing in the streets. They created giant mushroom clouds that turned their cities into burned out rubble. And worst of all, they did these things over and over again, exactly the same as they had done them the day before and the day before that. They never learned from their mistakes. Death by firing squad? No matter, show them the wall, give them a gun. A plane about to crash? Give them a seat. Icebergs? All aboard!

Just once, Ernesto wished they would stop in the middle of their mushroom-cloud building, their dancing in the rain, their disaster creating to stop and think. Do something new. Demand an end to the see-through insanity of the flat world.

Ernesto shifted in his seat, pushed away a stray clump of Patsy's fur and settled into his favorite sphinx position. Although he had never been able to prove it, he suspected that the flat people had been driven insane by the fact that their food had no taste and there was no escape from the flat world. He had first suspected this during his second night at the Palace when, excited by the salty appearance of a huge flat tuna flapping in the bottom of a small flat boat, he had leapt directly at the screen. His claws had hit the tuna and dug in as expected but when his weight dragged him down, ripping his claws through his prey, he had landed on the stage with nothing to show for his efforts. Looking up, he had seen the fish flapping exactly where it had been before his mighty leap, untouched in the bottom of the boat.

That same night, after the lights in the Palace came on and the audience had filed out of the lobby, he searched through the theater for any sign of the flat people but he found nothing. Behind the screen, the stage was empty. Downstairs, the dressing rooms were deserted. In the main hall, the screen, now marked with tiny claw tears, stretched silent and lifeless before empty seats. Was it possible the flat people had somehow sneaked out of the theater with the audience, taking their fish with them?

The next night at the Palace, a different audience had arrived, and even though Ernesto studied them carefully, he could not find a flat person among them. But when the lights went down and Steamer flicked the projector switch, the same flat people from the night before had appeared on the screen. With the same flat fish, they had moved forward, retracing their steps to a final drowning.

No wonder they were crazy.

Now, as he watched Steamer fiddle with projector knobs, he was beginning to think that flat people were so strange that they might not be real humans. Or was it possible that Steamer kept them prisoners in one machine and let them out onto the big screen only for exercise, like people did for dogs?

When the lights dimmed and the big screen flashed to life, Ernesto wanted to cry. But he did not know how. The same man and woman who earlier that morning had refused to eat even the smallest piece of chicken, not even a scoop of rice or a bite of kim chee, were once again acting as if food did not exist, as if staring into each other's eyes could produce the same sleepy happiness produced by a full stomach.

Poor things, Ernesto thought, closing his eyes. He did not want to see the start of another chase game that would end with these two starving flat people wrestling with each other in a soft bed as a mushroom cloud blossomed in the sky over their heads.

Ernesto closed his eyes and counted the seconds. Counted again. Instead of the usual heavy breathing followed by an explosion, he heard the peaceful lapping of waves against the shoreline. He pried open an eyelid and saw something he had never seen before. The mushroom cloud had been averted. In its place a stretch of beach played host to a man and woman locked together in a complicated wrestling hold, mouths biting at each other as the sky opened up and a girl riding a whale dove from the clouds.

"Wait a second," Steamer shouted. "Now watch."

The whale dove into the night, and a new woman appeared on the screen. Ernesto jumped up. The woman had her back to the camera, and it was too dark to see her clearly, but there was something familiar about her wide shoulders.

Fireworks exploded.

"Look!" Steamer shouted. "It's her!"

Under the red, white and blue shower of explosions, Mimi turned to the camera. She was standing on the roof of the Palace, waving to Ernesto.

For a moment, Ernesto could not move, then his heart leaped and with a shock he realized what he was seeing. Mimi was in the flat world, held prisoner in a world where food had no taste or smell. Where people and animals were forced to repeat themselves endlessly.

He jumped from his seat and charged the screen.

"Wait!" Steamer shouted. "Ernesto, come back!"

Ernesto ran at full speed, barely feeling his paws touching the sticky floor. She was up there, the woman. He would jump into her arms. Save her. Bring her back to the real Palace. He heard a string of explosions and saw her smile. He leaped over the orchestra pit, ricocheted off the organ, landed on the stage.

The screen went white.

Ernesto stopped an inch from where his claws had torn through the mysterious screen. She was gone. He sniffed the air, the stage, the screen. He smelled dust and mold but no woman. He searched behind the screen, sniffing every inch of wall and curtain. She was gone.

"Ernesto!"

The lights went up, and Steamer was running down the aisle.

Ernesto shot between the curtains and found the ladder that led to the roof. That's where he had seen Mimi in the flat world! She had been trying to send him a message. She was on the roof. He ran up the ladder and through Mimi's secret room into bright sunshine and ocean smell. This was the round world. The world with smells. He stopped at the edge of the roof and looked down at Angelica's home. Even from here he could smell the six kittens. They smelled delicious and real, like milk and cookies.

Mimi was here! He was certain because her ladder was still here, reaching from the Palace across the alley to Mr. Goodmorning's home. Ernesto had never seen anyone but her use it. No one else was brave enough. Where was she?

He heard crashing footsteps moving away fast over corrugated iron. Without thinking, he crossed the ladder, jumped to the fire escape, and climbed up its rusting ladder, the way he had seen Mimi do. He stopped, shifted his ears left and right, heard metal banging against the back of Mr. G's building, then a rubbish can rolling over concrete. He had never been this far from the Palace, and he was afraid, but he knew the chase game and how it started, so he followed the roof, his paws slipping in and out of the iron ridges, until he reached a ledge overlooking a strange alley.

Three flights down an old red pickup truck was backed into the shadows of a dead-end alley. A line of rubbish cans, one of them rolled over on its side, blocked the entrance to the street. From the window below him, a rusty fire escape zigzagged down to the alley. Ernesto checked behind him. If he wanted, he could be home in seconds. Then he heard the faint sound of human crying drifting up from the alley.

A dog barked.

Ernesto leaned forward, stretching his neck to see who was hiding behind the truck. Was that Mimi in the shadows? He tried to call her name, managed only a squeak. The crying stopped and the vague shape moved deeper into the shadows. Trying to dig his claws into the flimsy metal, Ernesto edged down a drainpipe, then pushed off and dropped to the fire escape. Holding his breath, he stepped lightly from one piece of shaky metal to the next, until he reached the last step, and jumped to the top of the truck.

"No," said a cry from the shadows.

The truck's red paint was faded and cracked, spotted with jagged rust holes, one of them bigger than Ernesto's paw. He was about to jump from the cab to the bed, when a voice behind him shouted, "How many times are we going up and down this street?"

A black car was blocking the alley and two men were standing on the sidewalk looking at a map. They were big men in loose fitting t-shirts and baggy shorts. Their white socks and swollen shoes were the kind people wore when they wanted to look like they were capable of running.

"I say we go back there and start knocking on doors."

"We will, don't worry."

They waved flies away and stepped away from the rubbish cans as Ernesto turned back to the shadows. He leaped down to the truck bed and ran to the tailgate. Standing on his hind legs, his front paws gripping rusted metal, he looked over the tailgate and saw bare feet.

He sniffed. Even from this far away, the feet smelled familiar. He leaned forward, inhaling mold and dirt and truck oil. Too late, the thought reached him that Mimi would not have smelly feet.

"I did it. I'll do it again!"

The bat whistled through the air and struck the truck's license plate. As Ernesto jumped to the top of the cab and slid down the windshield, he heard the Bopper shout, "Come back. I won't hurt you. Ernesto!"

The big men from the black car shoved the rubbish cans out of their way and stepped into the alley, blocking Ernesto's escape.

"What the hell was that?"

"Whose back there?"

There was no way around them except maybe along the wall and then a shot though the rubbish cans. As Ernesto was trying to think, an aluminum baseball bat skipped across the asphalt and skidded to a stop at the men's feet.

"What the hell!"

"A friggin bat?"

Ernesto felt the truck shake as the Bopper climbed into the bed. "Ernesto, see, no bat. Come back."

The bigger of the two men picked up the bat. He gripped it with two hands, and swung it twice, quick, high and low.

Ernesto jumped, landed on the wet concrete between the men and the truck. Behind him, the Bopper climbed up and onto the cab. Shoulders back, he waved the two men forward. Shoulders back, they stepped deeper into the alley, the seams of their shoes bulging. "Run!" the Bopper shouted, then waved to Ernesto and leaped into the air. He caught hold of the fire escape, and for a second his legs dangled.

"Crap," the man with the bat shouted as he cocked his arm. When he threw it, the bat sailed over

Ernesto's head, bounced off the truck, and hit the Bopper in the knee.

Ernesto ran. Afraid to look back, he dodged between white socks. Unlike the flat people, he told himself, he would learn from his mistakes. He would never again leave the Palace. Never ever. He heard a crash, closed his eyes, and leaped over the rubbish cans, into the rushing-car sounds of the street.

Chapter 8

S teamer stepped out of the Palace and stopped at the edge of what to him looked like an action movie gone bad.

In the street, Papa Joe was waving his arms and shouting, "Look out!" at a swerving car. A woman ran by him, scooped up a boy holding a grey cat, and somehow managed to stay ahead of the car until she reached the safety of the sidewalk in front of the Palace. She put the boy down and swatted him on the butt. The second swat popped Ernesto out of the boy's arms.

Iz

"Hey, be careful." Steamer said. "No need for violence."

As Papa Joe lumbered across the street, the woman picked up the boy, hugged and kissed him. Three times she kissed him on the forehead. Steamer thought he saw a tear in her eye.

"Hey Steamer, that boy is quick," Papa Joe said, squeezing the boy's shoulder. "You shoulda seen him grab Ernesto! Like a rocket that boy."

Steamer tried to remember his lines. He had not been outside for a few days and Papa Joe was talking fast, saying something about his boy Johnny and his wife Antonia and their boy, something about a cot and card table and no place for a woman and kid.

Steamer nodded. "Sure," he said. "Yes."

"Only for a couple of days," said Papa Joe, "until I can get some stuff moved around, make some room in the Empire."

Steamer checked the character list. Ernesto was okay. He had hopped back into the boy's arms and was trying to get inside his shirt. The boy was smiling. Papa Joe was talking. The woman was a woman.

"Mimi would be proud of you," Papa Joe said. "Doing a good deed. That's what she'd say."

Steamer pushed open the doors to the Palace, bathing the lobby in warm light. He wondered what he had promised. What he was supposed to do.

"My boy," Papa Joe said. "Johnny. He wants me to take care of them."

She was a young woman holding her boy's hand. The three of them were looking at him.

Ernesto too. "Welcome to the Palace," he said, stopping in the middle of the lobby and motioning them to follow. "Constructed in 1925, she was a Palace in the age of palaces."

The woman and boy looked at Papa Joe as he nodded, scratched his head, and Ernesto jumped to the floor, shot in and out of people's feet.

Say something, Steamer told himself, noticing that the woman was wearing a gold cross around her neck.

"Her redwood beams, each of them one foot thick," said Steamer, "made her for many years the strongest building in Hilo. And her stadium seating placed her on the cutting edge of technological design. I should point out that stadium seating offered in this venue did not become commonplace until more than fifty years later in the age of super malls and the multiplex."

Ernesto sniffed the boy's high tops.

Steamer knew this tour movie script by heart, had repeated it hundreds of times to tourists, grant auditors, and mildly curious donors. But today he was having trouble remembering the dates of the tsunamis, the closings, and the grand openings.

The boy reached down to pet Ernesto.

"And in a moment I'll show you one of our treasures, the Robert-Morton pipe organ. It was shipped here from Honolulu when the Waikiki Theater closed."

"This all good information," Papa Joe said to the woman. "Yes, this is a strong building. You don't have to worry here."

Steamer could see that the woman was still worried about the boy. She was holding him close to her, a firm grip on his shoulder. "You're very brave," Steamer said. "Both of you."

The boy picked up Ernesto and hugged him.

"I was showing him some home movies," Steamer said, "and he got scared."

"Scared of movies?" Papa Joe said. "Not Ernesto."

"Ten pounds," the boy said, lifting Ernesto into the air then setting him gently on the ground. "Maybe thirteen."

Steamer held out his hand and the boy shook it. He had a small hand but a vigorous handshake.

"Anthony," Papa Joe said. "Not Tony."

Steamer gave the boy a second look. "Doesn't look like an Anthony or Tony," he said.

"I was thinking the same thing," Papa Joe said. "And this is Antonia."

Steamer felt funny about shaking a woman's hand, so he picked up Ernesto and said, "Thank you for saving my cat. One of them." As he let Ernesto wiggle free, he added, "Did you notice the art-deco façade?"

"It is impressive," she said, both her hands on the boy's shoulders.

"Johnny lives in Honolulu," Papa Joe said. "Good kid."

Steamer wondered if Papa Joe had been drinking. Was that tequila he smelled? If Mimi were here, she'd be sniffing his breath. Wasn't there something on the list? Something about Papa Joe's drinking?

"We need a new roof," Steamer said. "Lots of work to be done. I have a list of repairs waiting for me."

"Johnny's a good worker. Maybe we can get him out here someday. To do some work."

Papa Joe said something about broken pipes and rusting roof panels while Ernesto jumped into the boy's arms and lay there, belly up, with his paws in the air, purring. He was quiet boy, and his mother was quiet woman, and because she was a woman, she reminded Steamer of Mimi. He looked at her and wanted Mimi to be home.

"We can get Teresa over here," Papa Joe said. "She knows how to swing a hammer. Maybe even Manny. Keep him away from hammers but he's good with a paintbrush. When he gets out of jail."

"I can fix things," the woman said.

The cross glowed on her skin, and Steamer was going to tell her how his friend Mimi was about her size, maybe a little bit bigger, and she could fix almost anything, when Papa Joe said, "I thought maybe you could put them up in the old dressing rooms."

"No way," Steamer said, moving toward the staircase. "Not even the cats can stand it down there. Too moldy. Need to put it on my list, my list of things to do."

While they climbed the stairs, he said, "Anthony, you watch out for Ernesto's claws. He looks kinda soft and cuddly but he's got hook claws."

"No need to worry about him," Papa Joe said. "That boy is smart. Perfect for around here. Keep your mind working. Fast on his feet."

Steamer pointed at the door marked *Men*. "Don't use the men's room. Got some problems in there. Have to jiggle the handle, can be tricky."

Papa Joe said, "There's a couple of big standup urinals in there. Biggest I've ever seen."

After a moment of silence, they stopped at the top of the stairs, and Steamer looked at the clock above the entrance to the balcony. It had stopped at 10. "It's been a long day," he said.

"That's Hilo," Papa Joe said. "Time moves slow."

"That means you will live longer," the woman said.

Steamer liked her name. Antonia. She was small boned, neat and clean. Was she younger than Mimi? Maybe the same age. "The Palace can seat 500 people. Each of the seats has a name on it. That was Mimi's fundraising idea. See, there?" He tapped the brass tag on closest seat. "See the tag. Amy Self. Her friend paid $25 for that nameplate."

"I know that girl," Papa Joe said, hand on the boy's shoulder. "Doesn't like to talk during the movie. Always hissing at people to be quiet. I sit over there, in the front row, out of her reach, second from the right, lots of leg room."

Steamer stood next to the woman and thought that Mimi would like that he was taking care of her and her son. The boy was small and fragile, but there must be something big inside him if he could run into the street and save a cat. Anthony, not Tony.

"The screen," he said, "can be raised up for stage performances. We've had thirty people on the stage for Hair,"

"Nude people," Papa Joe said. "Floor sags under that kind of weight."

"Impressive," said the boy.

The three adults eyed the boy, then Steamer pointed at the far wall. "There's a room upstairs. The door's over there, somewhere. Looks like the wall is solid but there's a door and an old pull-down ladder. Not many people know about it."

Ernesto jumped from the boy's arms and ran ahead of them.

"Only me and Mimi," Steamer said.

"And me," said Papa Joe.

"You?"

A few minutes later, after Papa Joe had finished his long and winding explanation of how Mimi had shown him the way just in case there was an emergency, Steamer climbed the last step of the ladder and crawled through the hatch. Ernesto was waiting for him, sitting by the room's only window, a picture window that opened onto the rooftops of Hilo and the volcano beyond.

"Keep it moving," Papa Joe shouted from below.

The boy popped through the hatch, the woman followed, and Papa Joe squeezed his shoulders through at an angle, saying, "Reminds me of my days in Amsterdam. I lived on the fifth floor next to a canal and had to climb the stairs three or four times a day. Was pretty strong in those days.

After a few months of that, I climbed all the way to the top of Cologne Cathedral."

Steamer listened and waited. He was used to chatter. Talk that filled up all the empty space was required in Hilo. Mimi had studied the phenomenon and determined that in Hilo every thirty seconds of important information was preceded and followed by at least five minutes of chatter.

"Me and Mimi came here all the time to read," he said, while thinking that something had changed. It was huge room and airy, with two folding chairs facing the window. Today it looked smaller. Her wine glass and open book sat on the blue-and-white cooler.

"Plenty room here," Papa Joe said. "Enough room for dancing."

"I doubt we'll be dancing," Steamer said.

"You can store food in your coffee table," Papa Joe said. "That's good. Tough to get stuff up here."

"You'll have to use the shower downstairs." Steamer said. "In the dressing rooms."

"Thank you," she said.

"No place for sleeping," Papa Joe said. "Need something for sleeping."

Steamer looked at the floor. It was solid and made of dark wood. "Yes, we need a bed."

"I like to sleep on the floor," the boy said.

Steamer showed them the door that led to the roof. Outside, a lounge chair and a stack of books sat in the middle of the small open space. There was just enough room for the four of them to stand under the roof overhang. Fresh air with a hint of salt and vog blew through on its way to the mountain. "We used to come up here all the time during the summer. We can haul up a couple of mattresses for you."

"It is not necessary," Antonia said, looking at the mountain, pushing her hair back.

Steamer saw the light on her neck as Papa Joe said, "Good for a boy to sleep on the floor. Makes him tough."

The boy sat in the chair, and Ernesto hopped into his lap.

Steamer wanted to say more, but he did not know what to say. He watched the boy pet Ernesto and thought about tomorrows. "Ernesto likes heights," he said. "Likes to hang his feet off the roof when he naps up here."

The boy squeezed Ernesto.

"Got to do something about beds," Papa Joe said. "Woman shouldn't be sleeping on the floor."

Steamer was certain this was true. "Stay away from that ladder over there," he said. "Mimi used it for keeping her eye on Mr. Goodmorning. Going to move it one of these days."

"Why's that ladder still there? No one can use that ladder," Papa Joe said. "Maybe I should pull it back now."

"I'll do it later," Steamer said. "Never know." He looked at the sky. "Could be hurricane weather."

"I do not think so," the woman said.

The five of them studied the sky.

From across the alley, Mr. Goodmorning shouted, "Good morning, neighbors." He leaned out of his window. "What you going to do about the kidnapping?"

Antonia put her hands on the boy's shoulders.

"Looks like a party over there, Steamer. You having a party?"

"No party. What kidnapping?"

"Don't have any parties without me."

"What kidnapping?" Papa Joe shouted.

"You seen it happen! You were out in the street playing with Patsy."

"I seen Patsy this morning," Papa Joe said. "She was heading up to the church but I didn't see no kidnapping."

The woman squeezed the boy's shoulders.

Steamer dug his hand into his pocket and felt a piece of round metal attached to frayed nylon. He looked at the ladder over the alley and then up at the sky. Dark clouds were racing across the blue, covering the sun, then setting it free. They reminded him of Mimi. He wanted to see her again. He wanted to hold her.

"One of Angelica's kittens is missing," Mr. Goodmorning shouted. "Rusty, he did it."

"That one mean cat," Papa Joe said to the boy. "You watch out for him. No manners, that cat."

"Patsy tried to stop him," Mr. Goodmorning said. "You should've seen her. She's one fighter."

"Patsy," Steamer whispered. Finally, the movie had jumped back on script. He knew what he had to do. "I have to find Patsy!"

Chapter 9

P atsy hid in her shelter under the mango tree and stared at Hilo Hospital. She was afraid of nothing, but this concrete building near the river made her heart beat faster. The biggest building in Hilo, bigger than the Pink Church, the Palace and the County Jail combined, the hospital was a concrete maze of crisscrossing hallways, prickly smells, and freezing temperatures.

Why Mimi came here so often, Patsy did not know. The woman would change into her white clothes, kiss Steamer goodbye, and then pedal her cruiser all the way up the hill with Patsy in the handlebar basket, just to disappear inside.

A full day and night later, she would reappear, still breathing, still herself but too quiet and too tired to coast all the way home without stopping twice to rest. First at the waterfall below the hospital, where she would nap in the mist. Then at the river's end, close to the Singing Bridge, where she would swim lazily across the deep black pools. Only then could she sit Patsy back in the handlebar basket and pedal the final few blocks home to Steamer and say, "Don't you ever go the hospital without me. That place will kill you. It's trying to kill me."

Patsy had been inside the hospital once, long enough to see and hear things that she did not understand and did not want to remember. No doubt, if she had stayed longer the hospital would have tried to kill her, but a man in a blue uniform had saved her. Wearing a badge like the guards wore at the jail, he had held up his hand and told Mimi to "March that cat right out of here!" Mimi had argued with him, even thrown her arms in the air, but when the man shook his head, she had finally told Patsy to go home, saying, "Heaven forbid the patients get a little love from a small animal."

Patsy had run away quickly, content to wait outside under the comfortable mango tree, where she napped and studied the comings and goings of people who were brave enough to enter the room called Emergency. None of them went in willingly. They staggered in or were pushed in on gurneys, and if they were lucky enough to escape, they came out in wheelchairs.

Was Mimi in there now? If so, Patsy would rescue her. She knew the quickest way in and would soon find the quickest way out.

She ran out of the shade and across the grass, hid under an ambulance. Breathing heavy, two men in black boots pushed a gurney toward the glass doors that Patsy knew would swing open magically. She slipped under the gurney, hopped on its steel ribs, and rode toward the Emergency.

"Whada yah think?"

"No insurance card."

"What? You think the Bopper has insurance?"

"He's busted up pretty good."

"Thirty, forty stitches will fix him up good. Guy's got a head like concrete."

"Not his head I'm worried about."

As the doors swooshed open, Patsy felt a blast of cold air that tasted of copper and disinfectant. The soft outside light turned into a white glare.

"Let's go look at the babies," a woman's voice said.

Patsy felt the earth shake. There were babies here? Who would bring a baby to such a place? She looked out from under the hanging sheet and saw two women in white uniforms following the gurney and drinking from red cans.

"If not babies, then let's go see Manny Matos."

"That man is crazy."

"He's an absolute saint of an angel."

"Manny?"

"Can't handle sugar. That's what gets him into trouble. Cute though, Manny."

"Manny Matos?"

When they turned, Patsy shot from under the gurney, switched directions and followed the white uniforms as they talked their way down a brightly lit hallway with a shiny, slippery floor.

"Coast Guard found him unconscious on his Sampan, 250 miles from land, no radio, no fuel. No telling how long he was out there."

"That man belongs in a jail."

"That's where he was before they brought him here."

They stopped in front of a small room guarded by a man wearing a badge and reading something called the Hawaii Fishing News. Patsy pressed herself flat against the wall as the women in white waved to someone inside.

"Hello, Doc."

"Hey, Doc, what you got there?"

"I got a Manny Matos."

"A Golden Madonna saved me," a familiar voice said.

"Sure, Manny. Hey, you give me a call when you get out of jail. Just ask for Nurse Jane."

"Never mind him, let's go see the babies."

Shaking their heads, the nurses returned to walking, white shoes squeaking on the tile floor, half whispering that the doctors had all the luck and the cop guarding the door looked like a winner.

As their voices faded, the guard watched them, and Patsy seeing her opportunity slipped inside the room and found a quiet spot under the bed. From there she could look out and see black high-top sneakers, a pink skirt, and the bottom half of a white lab coat. She peeked further out and saw that they belonged to Doc Trina.

Manny's voice said, "She came up, out of the sea, like a mermaid."

"Bandaged with duct tape?"

"Not at first. She had a cut on her neck and I fixed it up for her."

"How'd she get that?"

"Shrapnel. Said she'd been to a bad place and now she didn't want to go back. Lots of shooting. Came out my way to see peaceful water instead of sand storms. Said she heard my prayers and found me floating in the *Manila Queen*, looking like I could use some help."

The Doc clicked her pen and said, "Then what?"

"She showed me the crack in her neck and I patched her good. Duct tape can hold anything together."

"Cheap too."

"She told me to eat the Girl Scout cookies."

Doc Trina wrote something on a clipboard.

"I didn't want to because those cookies were for charity, but the Madonna said it was okay to eat a ton of them because she didn't like the Girl Scouts ever since they stopped selling Double Chocolate Zappers, which were her favorite. And because I needed to get back to Hilo. She wanted me to deliver a message to Steamer."

Manny got to talking so fast that Patsy could barely understand him. He said something about a fight in a bar and being worried about Steamer and staring at boxes of Cinnamon Twists and Ginger

Snaps and Peanut Butter Fingers and Sugar Scramblers. Finally, he took a quick breath and said, "Lucky she showed up."

"Who?"

"The Golden Madonna."

"Her again."

"Out in the ocean, alone, you need someone like that. I fixed her up and she calmed down the wind and rain. Made the thirty-foot waves flat, like in the Bible, so I could eat cookies and be her messenger. We didn't plan on me getting arrested."

"And these bruises on your back and ribs?" Doc Trina asked.

"You can't blame the Madonna for those."

The Doc put down her clipboard and moved closer to the bed. Patsy saw a piece of sugar cookie stuck in her shoelaces.

"Sit still," Doc Trina said.

Patsy heard bedsprings.

"Can't sit still. It's not my nature. Got to keep moving."

"You have to find a safer profession."

"Nothing safer than the sea."

Patsy ran from under the bed to under the chair next to the window where she could see Doc Trina peeling a bandage off Manny's shoulder and tossing it into a stainless steel rubbish can. "Yikes," she said, then quickly added, "Stitches don't look too bad. But you might have a scar."

"A man isn't much of a man without scars."

"Maybe you should get the Madonna to fix it. She might have extra duct tape."

"You making fun of the Madonna?"

"Of course not.

"Don't doubt the unknown, Doc."

Manny used his elbows to push himself up, and the Doc used her hand to push him down.

"You got to feel her," Manny said.

The Doc grabbed his wrist.

"Feel it here," he said, struggling to free his hand, finally getting it loose from the Doc's grip and pressing his finger against her chest. "In your heart."

"That's not my heart."

"But you feel things there, don't you?"

For a moment, the Doc and Manny were silent, holding hands and looking at each other. Patsy contemplated this silence and their staring, until the guard appeared at the door, asking, "You okay, Doc?"

"No problem here."

"You sure, Doc?"

Manny dropped back on the pillow, closed his eyes. "You're just looking out for me, right, Doc?"

The guard watched the Doc step back from the bed and pick up a syringe from a metal tray. "You can wait outside. I'm fine."

When the badge was gone, Manny opened his eyes. "What you got there, Doc?"

"I'm going to give you a shot for the pain," she said, loud and slow as if Manny was in the hall.

"Too much pain in the world, right, Doc."

"You rest. The police are right outside the door. You can't go anywhere. You understand?"

Patsy shrunk back as the needle entered Manny's skin.

He closed his eyes. "You're trying to help me. I know you, Doc."

The Doc pulled out the needle and rubbed Manny's arm with a cotton ball. "This will help you sleep."

"I'm not worried. I've seen the Madonna in plenty kine places. Even places like this."

"You're making yourself see things."

"Only way, Doc. Not going to see something you don't want to see. I even seen her at a club, a bar in Pearl City."

"What was she doing in a bar?"

"Working and keeping an eye on me. I was sitting in the corner watching the game and playing crossword puzzles with a couple of the girls, nice girls, hard workers, good dancers, and this guy walks in and plays "Witchy Woman" on the karaoke machine."

"Can't stand that song."

"Me too. Heard it too many times. Madonna didn't like it either."

"You're not supposed to be in bars."

"That's what the Madonna said. She came up to me and said I wasn't supposed to be in there. Said she wasn't supposed to be in there either. Said she'd get into trouble if you know who saw her."

"Who?"

"That's why she was wearing a disguise. This tight gold dress with a slit up the side."

"That's enough." Doc Trina turned toward the window, did something Patsy could not see. "Don't say another word."

"She said if the big guy saw her, she'd be in trouble so she was in disguise. Looked real pretty, like Mimi from the Palace, Steamer's girl, only with fancier shoes, those high heels they wear in heaven."

"Nice."

Doc Trina stepped away from the window, leaned over Manny. Patsy could not see what medical procedures the Doc was performing but she did see her whisper in his ear. Then the Doc rubbed his shoulder and stepped back, looked at her watch.

Manny closed his eyes.

"You sleep now, Manny. You'll be safe. The police are right outside." The Doc walked out and closed the door.

Patsy enjoyed shorts naps. She was closing her eyes when she heard the bed creak. The sheets fell to the floor and Manny's feet appeared, big and flat, landing on green linoleum tile. They walked directly to the window, with Manny's *okole* peeking out from his green gown as he pushed up the glass, knocked out the screen, and climbed onto the ledge. "Coming?" he said, then dropped to the ground.

Along a rocky trail that dropped almost too steep for a cat to follow, Patsy followed Manny to the bank of the Wailuku River. He had chosen a difficult path, one not even Mimi would take. To get to Hilo he would have to find a way down or around a series of rugged waterfalls. The air smelled of ginger and moss, banana and guava. A mist hung heavy near the ground. When Manny stopped to rest under a Banyan tree, Patsy climbed high into its branches and searched for signs of pursuit. Except for a stray dog and three pecking chickens, the trail was clear.

Below her, his eyes closed, Manny rested with his toes in the water. The river flowed past him, over rocks worn smooth, splashing toward a ledge that curled over and crashed down Rainbow Falls.

Manny opened his eyes and held a finger to his lips. "Don't say nothing."

Patsy blinked. How long had he known she was following him? As he climbed into the tree, she moved further up. Just to be safe, out of his reach. Manny was a friend but he was unpredictable. He sat on the branch below her, and they watched two boys in knee-length bathing suits slip and slide along the muddy trail. They were carrying six-packs of beer and beach towels.

"Listen, I got a message for Steamer," Manny whispered. "Me, I've been meaning to tell him but stuff's been happening."

The boys stopped at the ledge below the tree and spread their red-white-and-blue towels in the mud. They popped open two aluminum cans and guzzled beer, then looked over the ledge.

"Wannabe ghosts," Manny whispered.

The boys pretended to slip and fall, then threw their cans in the air and watched them drop into the churning water below.

"You seen the ghosts at the Ice House?" Manny whispered. "In that freezer where they took all the bodies after the tsunami?" You go out into the world, even on this river, you got to be prepared to see ghosts."

The boys popped open two cans each and raced to see who could drain them the fastest. They spewed beer and doubled over laughing, counting, "One, two, three."

Manny shouted, "Don't do it!"

Swaying, the boys looked into the tree. "Who are you?"

"The Madonna isn't going to like this," Manny said.

"You sitting in a tree with a cat?"

"She's a friend."

The boys laughed themselves to the ledge.

"If anything should happen to me, girl, you tell Steamer…"

The boys teetered at the edge, their wet feet slipping on smooth stone, beers still in hand. "One," they shouted. "One and a half." They leaned over. A little more, still laughing. And fell.

Quick as a cat, Manny climbed down the tree. Patsy crouched next to him, looking over the ledge. The water churned white and green and brown. Branches popped to the surface then disappeared. She thought she saw something bloated and brown caught in one of the whirlpools.

Manny shouted over the roaring waterfall, "You wait for me at the Singing Bridge." He did two deep-knee bends, crossed himself, and looked up at the sky. Then jumped.

lz

Chapter 10

Papa Joe had plenty jobs to

do. When the sirens faded toward the river, he shrugged off the heat and humidity and stepped into midday Hilo. He liked to walk just before sunset when the air was light and cool and the sun hidden behind clouds, but today he had no choice. He could handle the heat. He had work to do.

Steering toward the shop overhangs and their promise of shade, he walked with the letter from Johnny in his shirt pocket and Steamer's movie posters under his arm. "A woman is good," he said, walking faster to stir insights.

When none came, he looked for Patsy. He wanted to remember what it was like to be young and filled with desire. He wanted to understand, and she could help him.

Bay Front was her second home, and he was almost certain he would find her somewhere between the Palace and Manny's boat. That meant a mile or two of hard walking in thick damp heat. The sidewalk was deserted, so was the parking lot. Most of the stores were closed but there were nooks and crannies everywhere, and the playing fields were crowded with running children. Searching the town for cats and insights was hard work, but he would find her. If she wanted to be found.

He wiped heavy beads of sweat from his forehead and stopped in front of the Ocean Flower Surf Shop. He thought of the boy and how good it would feel to take him surfing. Through the window he saw the surfboard that Manny had warned him not to buy. In the old days the 10-foot Yater would have been made in Santa Barbara and weighed forty pounds. This beauty was made in Thailand and weighed less than ten pounds. Papa Joe had picked it up, felt its rails, and was ready to buy it until Manny said, "Un-American that board. You want one board made in Hawaii. One board with Hawaiian soul." Then he had promised to shape a perfect long board for him. That was six months ago.

Papa Joe imagined his back not hurting when he picked up the un-American board and walked into the water with the boy. He would show him the small break by Singing Bridge and teach him how to avoid the dead reef. But if he wanted to go surfing while the boy was still a boy, he would have to buy this board in the window. "Manny is a good shaper and a good friend," he said to the surfboard, "but he's too good at finding trouble." He dug a small roll of duct tape out of his pocket. "And when he gets into trouble who knows where he will end up and when he will return."

He taped a movie poster and a missing-cat flier to the surf-shop door. Then he walked past the candy store and the t-shirt shop. He didn't need candy or t-shirts. Then he walked back and taped a missing-cat flier to the candy store wall and a movie poster to the T-shirt window.

Did the boy like candy? Even boys who knew candy was bad for them liked candy. Would his mother let him eat candy? She was a good woman and would understand the importance of candy. He stopped at the Lizard Mama store. Through the open door, he studied the neatly arranged shelves lined with bolts of Japanese silk and rice-paper lamps. On the floor, there were stacks of thick futons. In the back, a whole room full of hardwood cabinets, half of them handmade in Japan, the other half handmade in Korea to look as if they had been handmade in Japan. All good stuff.

For a long moment he inspected the overstuffed futons. They were not like the futons at the big stores on the road to the mall. These futons were made of the finest recycled cotton, stuffed and packed tight into the finest grade, smoothest canvas. They would last forever, and they were good for sleeping. A boy and his mother needed plenty sleep. A Japanese lamp, two pairs of thick cotton bedroom slippers, and a Korean cabinet with secret drawers would also be helpful for sleeping.

Finding a good bed for the woman was important but Papa Joe understood the logistics of work. He stuck a missing cat flier on the wall, next to a poster for free swimming lessons in the Wailuku River, and told himself he would return this way for the futon, no matter what. If possible.

He walked past the health food store and the restaurant named after a spaghetti sauce. He checked every table for Patsy. She had friends here and often came here to listen to jazz on Sunday afternoons, but it was too early for jazz and Patsy was not inside. Across the street the ocean was smooth as glass, a sure sign that a storm might or might not be approaching.

Surprised, he stopped at Reuben's Cantina. Usually, its doors were closed on Sunday but today they were open. Teresa was sitting at her favorite table under the matador poster while her mop and broom leaned against the wall.

"Hey, Joe," she called. "Come sit with me."

Papa Joe looked at the pitcher of on-the-rocks margaritas in front of his friend. Teresa was the best waitress in town and always poured extra-strong margaritas. Today she was reading the Sunday paper and sitting at the only table in the restaurant with an ocean view. In her t-shirt and jeans, she looked strong and professional and capable of much searching and duct taping.

"How about a drink?" she called. "On me."

"I got work to do," he said, stepping inside. He checked under the table, the cool spot where

Patsy liked to sleep and wait for tasty scraps and stray cockroaches.

"What you looking for down there?"

"Got a job to do."

"What kine job?"

A small dog wandered in, sniffed around for stray chips, and sat down in the corner near the door. Papa Joe stared at the dog, and the dog stared back. For a small dog, he looked capable of great actions.

"Seven, maybe eight pounds," Papa Joe said. "Can't go anywhere in Hilo without seeing a dog."

Teresa lit a Lucky Strike and exhaled a cloud of smoke at the open door. "Or hearing one bark. Some kine weenie-dog mix, this guy." She pointed her cigarette at the dog and said, "Out!" The dog left in a hurry, and Teresa picked up the pitcher of margaritas. "Have a drink."

Papa Joe shook his head. "Not today."

"What?" she said, setting the pitcher down closer to him. Going back to work on her Lucky Strike, she inhaled then holding her breath. "Cannot be."

"No drink for me."

"You're turning down a free margarita?" She exhaled. "On a Sunday afternoon?"

"I got work to do." He was thinking that the dog might have helped to find Patsy but then he remembered that Patsy was smarter than any dog.

"What kine work?" Teresa kicked off her rubber slippers, stretched her legs so that her bare toes pointed at Papa Joe.

Papa Joe looked at the pitcher of margaritas, at the empty chair across from Teresa.

"What kind work?" she asked.

"I got these posters to put up." He spread a movie poster on the table so that Teresa could see it.

"That's Bogart in Casablanca," she said. "I seen it a hundred times at the Palace."

"This time it's different."

Steamer had crossed out •*lanca* and scribbled in *Noir*. Under that he had written *Fatal Desire* and under that in small print *Whales in Paradise*

"CasaNoir?" She pushed an empty glass at him. "What's that mean?"

Papa Joe shrugged. "Something about dark houses."

"Does it have a happy ending?"

"I think so. No telling with Steamer."

"Put it on the wall over there. Everyone will see it."

Papa Joe duct-taped the poster at eye level under the matador.

"Is that a whale?" Teresa asked. "I have never seen a whale before in Casablanca. They got whales in the Mediterranean?"

"It's an ocean. Must have whales."

"What's that down in the corner?"

"Patsy."

The two of them looked at the stick-figure cat complete with whiskers above a note in blue ink saying, "Patsy is missing! Call the Palace!"

"We got to talk to Steamer," she said. "Get him back to being Steamer."

Papa Joe sat next to her, his back to the bar so he could see the ocean. It was out there, on the other side of the bandstand and the road. "Nothing wrong with sitting," he said.

"Sitting is good."

She poured him a drink, and they sat shoulder to shoulder. The smell of tequila and Teresa made him remember an insight. She was a hard worker, and he liked hard workers. He liked how she never drank before her work was done, and how when she drank she smiled and laughed and only rarely got into fights. It was good for a man to know a woman. He took the letter from his pocket. "I figure this letter weighs two or three pounds."

"Got some reading to do?"

"This letter."

"Read," she said, lifting the newspaper and giving it a backhand slap. "I'm not stopping you. All kines reading in here for me." She spread the paper on the table. "Jeezsus, I can't believe this." She tapped the paper. "Look at this."

Papa Joe squinted at the black-and-white photo and remembered the headlines he had been reading that morning with Patsy. He had avoided the photo then, and he avoided it now. Quickly, he looked back at the letter. He had seen enough bodies.

Teresa inhaled smoke, said, "Club Two Time. In Pearl City. I know that club. Nice place. I don't remember no bushes. You know the place?"

"Been to lots of clubs."

Papa Joe spread his letter on the table as Teresa peered through cigarette smoke. "Manny," she said, "he likes that club."

Papa Joe did not have time to think about Manny. Trying to smooth out the creases, he rubbed his hand over the letter, waited for insights from the feel and smell of the paper. When none came, he started reading.

Uncle, you kept me out of trouble when I was a kid, so maybe you can get me out now. I'm asking for Antonia, not me. She didn't have any choice in this. Lots of the guys around here think I'm crazy. So be it. They don't mean nothing to me. She means everything.

Anyway, you need to know how it started.

Back before I met her I was working construction. Eight hours hanging dry wall, cash at the end of the day. No taxes. Another four hours behind the bar at Club Two Time, in Pearl City. You know the place, you been there. Kinda mix between a hostess bar and a strip club. Loud with pool balls and music and you come home smelling like chili and rice and cheap perfume but good money. I shared a place with two bedrooms with a couple of guys from the Big Island. We split the rent, me paying fifty bucks less because I got the couch. That's all I needed.

Honolulu's not bad if you don't mind a big city and lots of people. I was working. That was good, Joe. Having two jobs and making money.

*Except you know how it is. A guy
gets to staring at the walls and wanting
something and sometimes he doesn't even
know what it is.*

*I worked at the bar until 2 or 3 in
the morning. Had a few drinks, went home
to sleep and woke up a couple hours later
to pound nails. The next day I did it all
over again. I stayed busy, so busy I was
saving money. Enough to look around at
the guys at the bar and ask myself
questions. The guys were laughing and
drinking and then going home to their
wives and kids. They had a place, a
home. It made me think.*

*I didn't figure a guy could get lonely
in Honolulu, but around three to five in the
morning if a guy can't get to sleep, things
get plenty lonely. It's quiet, real quiet even
with all the noise. You can understand
that, Joe, can't you? What it's like being
alone when you're young?*

*Anyways, the guy who runs the
club one night he needs someone to walk
him out to the car because he's carrying
money. You know Pearl City at night, so I
go, and we're walking out to the car and a
couple of punks they come out of nowhere
and before I know it, they're holding a
knife on me and the club guy.*

"Look at this, Joe," Teresa nudged him with
her elbow.

A white Mustang with cop lights on top had parked in front of Reuben's. Leaning out its window, a young cop in uniform shouted, "Hey Joe, you seen Manny Matos?"

Papa Joe had seen the cop before, snooping around the Palace when Mimi was still in town. "I hear you got him at the jail."

"We took him to the hospital and he escaped. Don't know where he is now."

Teresa poured herself a drink. "Never heard of no one escaping from that hospital," she said.

Chapter 11

E rnesto let the small boy lift him off the ground. He liked being held by Anthony even though the boy had tiny hands with skinny fingers that poked into Ernesto's ribs.

"Ten pounds," the boy said.

Pressing his body against Anthony's chest, Ernesto worried that the boy was too thin and fragile for life in the Palace. He had no weight, no padding, no width. One missed meal and the boy would fall into the flat world.

"As soon as I get some food in you," Steamer said, "I'll check around town for Patsy." He was standing next to the stove, holding an empty frying pan that should have been filled with sausages and eggs. "I'll be back in plenty of time for the movie. Sit over there."

The boy sat down at the table and Ernesto rearranged himself to fit snuggly in his tiny lap. He wondered if anyone was going to cook rice. A boy this thin needed rice. And tuna fish. And chicken sausage fried in butter.

"You're a big guy," Steamer said. "You like cookies?"

The boy nodded, and Ernesto realized he was a smart boy.

Steamer set the frying pan on the stove and tossed the boy a bag of Oreos. "These will hold you until I can get breakfast moving. They're one of Ernesto's favorites."

The boy opened the bag and selected a promising cookie. With nimble fingers he twisted it in half, leaving a thick layer of sweet white stuff stuck to each chocolate disk. He placed one on the table in front of Ernesto and said, "Sugar is good for you."

Ernesto licked the Oreo. The boy was small and fragile but he knew the rules of nutrition and was willing to share. The sugar rushed through him as he watched the boy break the other half of the cookie into two pieces, stick them together, and fit them into his mouth. He was a good eater. Ernesto could tell by the way he made the cookie disappear without the aid of milk.

Steamer moved the frying pan to a new burner, moved it back to the original. He leaned into the light from the window, looked up at the sky, and opened his mouth to say something. No words came out. He was still standing there looking up at the light when the woman walked into the snack bar.

"Let me help," she said, taking the plastic bag from the boy and the frying pan from Steamer.

Ernesto was disappointed in the boy. He had made no effort to keep the remaining cookie. Now Steamer was holding the bag and looking at it as if he didn't know what to do. Finally, he put it in the cookie drawer where it would be unable to feed any hungry people. The woman should have given the bag to Ernesto. He knew what to do with cookies.

"Anthony must not eat too many cookies," she said, touching Steamer's elbow, moving him gently away from the stove's burners. "Boys do not always know when to stop."

Ernesto was proud of the boy's reputation for cookie eating. He heard violin music coming from the boy's pocket. He liked violins. He licked what was left of the Oreo as the woman turned on the burner and found a carton of eggs in the refrigerator. He wanted to tell her to look deeper inside. There was rice, ham, and cheese hiding in there. All good for frying.

How she did it, he did not know, but like Patsy she heard his thinking. She went back to the refrigerator and dug deep inside until she found a hunk of ham and a bag of brown rice.

While she filled the rice cooker, Steamer sat at the table and rubbed his eyes. Ernesto thought that the man must be so hungry that the tightness in his stomach was squeezing tears from his eyes.

Fueled by sugar, Ernesto felt an idea bloom, and he encouraged its growth by licking more cream off his Oreo. Steamer was trying to starve himself into the flat world. He was treating food as the flat people did, avoiding it except for a sip of chocolate milk and a nibble of popcorn so he could become one of them and enter the flat world to save Mimi. Ernesto wanted to go with him but he doubted his ability to starve himself into thinness. He was weak and undisciplined.

Still licking his cookie, he worried. Soon the man would be no thicker than an Oreo. The boy and his mother were already flat enough to make the journey. If they ventured into the flat world with Steamer, would they find Mimi and return? Or would they be lost forever?

Ernesto watched the woman chopping onions and tomatoes, cutting off a thick slab of butter and tossing it into the pan. His love for her bloomed as the smell of frying butter spread through the room.

A cat could not live on cookies alone.

The woman tossed the onions and tomatoes into the pan, and Ernesto's heart rose upward with the cloud of sizzling music.

"Smells good," Steamer said, looking into the frying pan, standing close to her, shoulders almost touching. "Just make enough for you and the boy. I'm not eating"

"Please, go and sit down," the woman said, recognizing madness when she saw it. "You must eat."

The man did as he was told, and Ernesto was pleased to see the woman quicken the pace of cooking. But if the woman wanted him to eat, did that mean she did not want him to venture into the flat world? Was she trying to stop him from saving Mimi?

"Do you have corned beef?" she asked.

"Somewhere in the shelves."

Top right, Ernesto said. Who could live without corned beef? Only the people in the flat world.

"What movie are you showing tonight?" she asked, rummaging through the cabinets.

"*CasaNoir*."

"I have not heard of it."

She found the red can, pried the key off the bottom, and worked the can open without difficulty. She had experience and skills. The more Ernesto saw of this woman, the more he liked her.

"Have you heard of *Casablanca*?

"Everyone has heard of *Casablanca*." She cracked open an egg, one-handed, dropped it in the pan, and tossed the shells into the sink.

"Well, my movie is part *Casablanca* and part *Whale Rider*, cut up and mixed together." The man was talking fast, like he did when he talked to Mimi in the mornings after their wrestling matches. Ernesto closed his eyes and started to purr. "I don't mean influenced by these films," Steamer said. "I mean actually cut up and remixed together, with some old Hong Kong karate films thrown in to satisfy the trustees. They like movies with subtitles."

What is *CasaNoir* about?"

"That's only the working title. I'm also thinking about *Fatal Desire*. It's an anti-war movie."

"I see."

The eggs sizzled.

"Casablanca will start and then the Whale Rider will appear. It's tricky, I still need to polish that part. But I know this. Instead of getting on that plane to go fight Nazis or walking into the desert, no one is going anywhere. Everyone stays put, and no one gets killed."

Ernesto opened his eyes and saw the woman use the black spatula to scoop eggs, corn beef and onions onto a plate. She was a good woman. "Who will kill the Nazis?" she asked.

"I haven't figured that out yet." Steamer looked at the floor, the brass-plated cash register, and the plastic popcorn machine. "But I refuse to show a movie that romanticizes suffering. I'm going to have the Whale Rider save Bogie, Ingrid Bergman, and the audience."

Antonia placed two plates on the table, a big one for the man and a smaller one for the boy. They were piled high with corn beef and scrambled eggs. "The rice is still cooking," she said, looking at Steamer. "Will many people come to your movie tonight?"

"Most people go to the multiplex at the Plaza," Steamer said. That's our mall. But we have a loyal following of twenty or thirty. Plus the trustees coming over from Oahu to check on me. Maybe Papa Joe can get a few more with our posters."

While he waited for the woman to bring him a plate, Ernesto watched her closely, trying to see through her, like he could see through the flat people. Without getting food for herself or a hungry cat, she sort of sat down next to Steamer. She seemed to be only half sitting in her chair, half of her ready to run. Was she playing the chase game? Did she know any wrestling holds? She was too thin to pin a player but she looked quick and agile enough to use Ernesto's method of slipping out of any hold her opponent tried to apply.

"When you're through eating," she said, "can you show me your movie?"

"No need to wait." The man stood up, took her hand and led her through the lobby toward the stairs. Ernesto wanted to stay in the snack bar but the boy picked him up in his fragile arms and followed his mother.

They climbed the stairs, and he sat with the boy in the back row while Steamer and the new woman worked in the projection booth. Still hungry, Ernesto settled into the boy's boney lap and closed his eyes. He liked being warm. He liked sleeping. He liked eating more but if the man could starve himself into the flat world, so could Ernesto.

He purred, dreaming of fried chicken skins. He dreamed long and hard in oblong loops that went in and out of a wonderful world under a cloudless sky, where Mimi's strong but delicate hands were rubbing his neck and feeding him Crispy Pork Rinds manufactured in Honolulu.

An explosion woke him.

On the screen, a group of flat people holding guns huddled around a boiling pot of thick stew. Happy and smiling, they dipped huge chunks of white bread into thick gravy. A shell exploded, and for a moment the screen went dark.

Something close to sadness dug into Ernesto's stomach. Had the stew survived? Without letting them know he was leaving, Ernesto slipped to the floor. He could not stand the sight of food, even flat world food, being destroyed by explosions. Lightly he stepped across the sagging wood.

In the projection booth, he heard Steamer tell the woman, "I want to cut that out. See, here, I've got a nice piece with some karate guys and Bogie with Lauren Bacall."

Ernesto found the hole in the wall behind the stack of old film posters. He stopped, listened. Heard Chinese voices, then a woman with a raspy voice say, "You know how to whistle, don't you?" He looked back and watched the new woman touch Steamer's arm while he worked at the keyboard.

Ernesto squeezed through the mouse hole and stepped into sunlight streaming from tall windows.

The sheets and pillows that Steamer and Mimi used for wrestling games were scattered on the wood floor. He smelled the man on the sheets, and somewhere far away, hidden deep in the shadowy world of many yesterdays, he smelled her, the woman Mimi. He would starve himself into flatness and help the man find her. If only he could train himself to not fear stew-killing explosions.

He tried not to think about food. If it were raining, Patsy and Mimi would be here with him, and they would huddle under the covers, listening to the rain on the tin roof and the man downstairs pounding nails. On such days, the woman could make treats appear magically.

Ernesto leaped onto the dresser, stepped over the picture of the man and the woman drinking margaritas at Reuben's restaurant. Roasted meat, rice and beans beckoned to him brightly colored plates.

The top drawer was open, and he surveyed its promising landscape. Before jumping in, he sniffed the air. The drawer smelled familiar and friendly. He landed on silky material, dug through the holes, and hooked his claws into a cotton t-shirt. When he pulled back, the moving t-shirt revealed an envelope. With his nose, he pushed the envelope out of the way and found underneath it a packet of his favorite treats: Extra-Salty Tropical Tuna Tidbits.

He clawed at the bag, holding it steady with one paw while he ripped at it with the other. Inside, the frightened fish were packed in tight, seeking safety in numbers. He bit the end of the package, ripped, and inhaled the salty goodness. Hooking his claw into the hole his tooth had made, he ripped open the package. Salty treats flew in all directions. One landed on the t-shirt. Another on a pair of her socks.

He ate as he searched. One treat found, one eaten. Under Mimi's string of black beads, he found another fleeing fish. Ate again and again, until the school of frightened tidbits had been scientifically thinned.

He stretched out full length in the drawer, feeling cool and warm at the same time. Then he curled into a ball, back paws holding front paws, tail tucked in, head resting on a perfect pillow – a fluffy stack of the woman's cotton underwear.

Chapter 12

S teamer was ready again to try the world outside the Palace. He stepped out the front door and held it open for the boy.

"Enough talk about movies," he said. "We got work to do."

The boy saluted him, a snappy salute Steamer had seen the British use in the movies. As the little fellow passed him, Steamer heard Vivaldi leaking from the boy's earphones. "Before we go anywhere," he told the boy, "I have to tell you a few things. Help to keep you safe."

The boy stopped, and Steamer sniffed the air. "Got to watch the air in Hilo," Steamer said, and slapped his chest. "All kine bad air blows here from the volcano."

The boy sniffed left and right.

"Almost good today," Steamer said.

"Almost good," said the boy.

"Not that Hilo is a dangerous place. But it can be dangerous." He jerked his backpack high and tight on his shoulders. "Got some weight here."

The pack held two coffee-table books big as coffee tables, sixteen scrambled eggs in an airtight container, twenty-four packages of ramen noodles, three bottles of Tapico hot sauce, and five cans of Spam (50% less fat). "If Papa Joe were here he could tell us exactly how much this baby weighs," Steamer said to the boy, who had his own load to carry.

"Ten pounds," the boy said, jerking his small green book bag high on his shoulder. Three packages of Oreos (double cream) protruded from the top of the faded bag.

"Now listen," Steamer said.

The boy turned off his music.

"There are a few things you need to know to stay out of trouble in Hilo."

A dog barked.

"That's the first thing. Everyone on this island except me owns a dog. Everywhere you go, you're going to hear a dog barking. Can't do nothing about it. Some of them been chained up all day and left alone, so they bark and get mean. Stay away from them, especially the big ones. Others just bark because they are dogs and dogs are meant to bark."

"Goodmorning, neighbor!"

"The same goes for that skinny guy up in that window," Steamer said softly, only half caring if Mr. Goodmorning heard him. "You can't go anywhere without him seeing you. Makes lots of noise. But forget about complaining. It won't help." Steamer pushed the Oreos deeper into the boy's bag.

"Say hello to everyone. Look them in the eyes. Unless they're pissed off, then don't look them in the eyes. Unless you like beef."

"I do not like to fight," the boy said.

"Good."

"Unless I am forced to."

"Well, okay" Steamer said. The boy was more complicated than he had thought. "But no one can force you to fight."

"Goodmorning, neighbor!"

The boy looked up at Mr. Goodmorning and waved. Mr. Goodmorning waved back, shouted, "That's a good boy you got."

Steamer turned the boy toward the street. "And don't act like you're smarter than anyone. That'll get you in real trouble."

The boy smiled.

"Mostly," Steamer said, "just look friendly." He locked the door to the Palace, bent down and grabbed the boy under the arms, lifted him a few feet off the ground, waited for his weight to stretch him out. When he set him back on the ground, he said, "Always good to look bigger than you are. Walk straight but humble."

Steamer turned around and stepped onto the sidewalk, saying over his shoulder, "Most important, don't talk to tourists. They ask too many questions."

"Good advice," said a stranger's voice.

Steamer stopped in time to avoid running into the wide back of a big man holding a digital camera above his head while he pointed it at the Empire. He had thick black hair, a scar on his neck, and smelled of hair oil. "Tourists," he said, and clicked a picture, "are some crazy people."

A black car was parked at the corner. The sky had turned an ugly grey.

"You should see Waikiki," the big man said, turning to Steamer. He was wearing dark glasses, a blue golf shirt stretched over a bulging stomach, Bermuda shorts, white socks, and running shoes. "Plenty tourists over there. Too many and too crazy. We like Hilo better."

Steamer touched the list in his pocket. He had important things to do.

"Shane," the man said, "like in the movie." He pointed at the car. Another big guy was squatting in the driver's seat. "Me and my buddy are over for a couple days. Then we're going to Maui."

"I'm Steamer. And this is Anthony."

The man looked behind Steamer. "Who?"

"Anthony," Steamer said, but when he looked back, the boy was gone. "Not another one."

"You lose something?"

Steamer nodded. "Got to add him to the list."

"Funny place Hilo," the man said, shaking his head. "Mind if I shoot a couple pictures of those doors? Haven't seen doors like that in ages." The man pointed his camera at the box office, pressed once. Pointed the camera at Steamer, pressed once. Waited. Pressed again. "Me, I got plenty of shots of the church, the pink one, and the jail up the road. Lots of grainy stuff. Mold on the concrete. Stuff like that. Ghost town pictures. That's Hilo, right. A ghost town. Like this old theater."

Steamer thought of all the ground he had to cover. Patsy could find her way back, but where was the boy? He had tiny legs but was quick, like a cat. Still, he couldn't have gone far. "You from the ship?" he asked the man, not caring about the answer.

"The ship? Oh, yeah, the cruise ship. I haven't been on a ship since my Navy days. Wouldn't get me on one of those again. Had enough of that. Wish I had a camera in those days."

The big tourist took two more pictures of the Empire.

"Well, goodbye," Steamer said, fingering the nylon collar in his pocket. "Got to look for my cat. Patsy. Named after Patsy Mink."

"Cats!" The man clicked off a couple more shots of Steamer. "Plenty of cats around here. I seen them all over. You shoulda seen the one we saw in the alley back there."

"Kinda solid?" Steamer asked. "With two blue eyes and a brown mask and a white tip on her tail?"

"Nope. Sounds like a nice cat. How'd you lose her? Girl cats, usually they hang around, stay close to home."

"This one wanders."

Steamer felt himself sinking in the quicksand of street life in Hilo. A rough breeze started up from the bay, and he smelled diesel fuel and aftershave. Where was the boy?

"You live here?" the man asked.

"Kinda."

"Never heard of no one kinda living in a movie house." He pulled a Milky Way from his shirt pocket, ripped opened the wrapper with his teeth.

"Gotta go," Steamer said, checking both ends of the street.

The tourist was in his way, pointing a candy bar at the movie poster duct-taped to the box office window. "This what you got showing tonight?"

Steamer looked at the alley.

"Never heard of *CasaNoir* but it looks good." The man shot two pictures of the poster. "What's the whale rider girl doing in there?"

"Giving it a new ending."

"I like happy endings. Like it better when the boy gets the girl, you know what I mean? Can't remember, does Bogie get the girl in *Casablanca*?"

"Kinda." Steamer stepped toward the alley, but the tourist grabbed his arm.

"What you mean *kinda*?"

"He keeps her love but she goes away to be with her husband and fight the Germans."

"Germans always causing trouble."

Steamer looked up at Mr. Goodmorning's window. He was up there watching, resting on his elbows. Steamer called to him, "Did you see the boy?"

"No boy around here."

The tourist bit into the candy, talked while he chewed. "Hey, not to change the subject but..." He pulled Steamer to the edge of the sidewalk. "You see that place over there? The Empire? Can you help me with something?"

Steamer remembered Mimi's lectures about the way he was supposed to treat tourists. You have to remember that they are people, she had told him over and over. He wondered if that included the ones ate sticky candy and grabbed his arm while the boy was probably heading for the ocean?

"Only a second," Steamer said. "I got a list of things to do."

"Me, too. I got a list. First, I'm trying to find an old friend. Said if I made it to Hilo, I should look him up. Big guy, kinda slow, used to be in the navy. A couple hundred pounds, maybe 250, about my size, maybe bigger. Supposed to live in a place called the Empire."

"Papa Joe?"

"Sure, that's right. Joe was his name. Last I heard he was living out here in Hilo. We're old friends. I think that store over there is the place I'm looking for. You know when he's going to get back? This Papa Joe?"

"He comes to all my movies."

The tourist looked at the poster. "Tonight at 7:30?"

"7:30."

"That's right, I remember that now. He likes movies. I remember."

Steamer moved toward the alley, and the man followed him, saying, "I'll be here. Me and my buddy, we like movies."

Steamer checked behind the dumpster and found a trail of Oreo cookies leading to Angelica's home.

The man looked behind the dumpster. "Cats," he said. "Looks like you got new kittens."

"Yes, kittens."

"Did I tell you that I seen a cat earlier?"

"Goodmorning neighbor."

A dog barked.

The tourist looked up, waved at Mr. Goodmorning, and Mr. Goodmorning shouted, "Go away!"

"Easy there, Tiger," the tourist said, then turned to Steamer. "Your friend is going to hurt himself, hanging out a window like that."

"I got it on the list."

"What list?"

"A list of good deeds."

The man laughed, and said, "Hey, let me ask you something?" He took a hold of Steamer's shoulder. "Is Joe living alone these days? Back in the day he was one fast guy with the ladies."

Steamer could not imagine Papa Joe doing anything fast. Except maybe swimming. Papa Joe was a fast swimmer for an old guy. "Living alone," Steamer said.

"No wife, huh?"

"Lives alone."

"Not even a girlfriend. Papa Joe he always had one girlfriend.

"Steamer, get up here," Mr. Goodmorning shouted.

The tourist kept a hold on his arm.

"He has a friend," Steamer said. "A waitress at Reuben's."

"The Mexican place up the road?"

"But she doesn't live with him."

The man let him go and walked to the rental car. His friend leaned over and pushed open the passenger-side door. He was wearing the same tourist uniform, and there was no space between him and the steering wheel.

"My buddy in the car, he's getting over a tough divorce. Tough break. You know what I mean? Thought Joe might know someone who could help take his mind off it." He threw his candy wrapper in the street.

Steamer picked up the wrapper, checked the street for the boy, checked the empty lot next to the Empire. It was the middle of the day, on Hilo's main street, and these tourists had somehow escaped from a bad television show, and somehow he had lost the boy a few feet from the Palace. He wished he had a baseball bat. No, no the boy might see him. But he had lost the boy. He had things to do, a cat and a boy to find.

"Know any place we can meet some nice women?" the driver asked.

Steamer tossed the candy wrapper in the rubbish can. He knew what he wanted to say.

The camera boy got in the car and slammed the door. "Oh well, just checking," he said. "Hey, do me a favor, will yah, don't tell Joe we stopped by. Maybe we can surprise him. You know, old war buddies."

The man said something else as the car drove away, but Steamer didn't hear him. He was looking for the boy and listening to the wind blow through the telephone lines.

Chapter 13

P atsy considered the sleeping beer drinker. His feet were in the water, his head on dry land, and he was smiling as if he were dreaming.

"My, my, a miracle. How did this get here?" Manny said, dragging a rowboat from the cover of a ginger patch. "Complete with lunch and sentry."

Patsy smelled beer and blood.

"Never mind him. That boy will be fine once he learns how to hold his booze." Manny tugged the boat into the water, dropped under, and popped up, shaking himself dry like a dog.

"Lucky my friend Big Black was on duty," he said, stepping onto dry land. "Without him on the job, this thing would have been stolen long ago. No doubt."

In the bow, Big Black was curled in a knot, eyes closed, and snoring.

"Like I was saying…" Manny stepped into the boat and sat down facing the stern. From under the seat, he pulled a small blue-and-white cooler and dug out a cheese sandwich. "If anything should happen to me…" He ate the sandwich in three bites and chased it with a big bottle of Hawaiian Spring Water. "You got to tell Steamer a message. We don't want him to end up like the people who jump off that bridge over there."

Patsy looked across the pool at the Singing Bridge. Cars rushed by in both directions, making the metal hum.

"Believe me, I seen it happen. I got plenty experience in these matters."

Patsy stared at him from shore. His legs were sticking out from a wet hospital gown, and his knees and shins were bleeding.

"You can't blame me for what happened. Restless as a cat, that woman of yours. You tell Steamer not to worry. The Madonna says she's living in a better place. The happily ever after."

With a paw on the boat, Patsy hesitated. She did not know if she wanted to go to sea with a man who had jumped off a waterfall in a hospital gown, but he had saved the two boys and now he had said something about where the woman was living.

Patsy leaped into the skiff. As Manny dug the oars into the water, she ducked between his legs and under the seat. Jumping from the thick green water in the bottom of the boat, she landed on a dry spot next to Big Black. He moved his tail to make more room for her.

"You make a nice couple," Manny said, pulling the oars through the shallow water.

Patsy bent close to big Black's nose and felt his long slow breathing. He was an old cat with black hair bleached orange by the sun and salt water. His only white spot, a huge star on his chest, was dark with dirt, and his long thick hair was matted with tiny clumps of fish guts. Patsy liked him because he was a music lover. Whenever Manny's boat was in harbor, Big Black spent his days on the dock and his nights behind Pesto's, swinging his bushy tail to the rhythm of three-piece jazz. He was slow and heavy, but he was also tough and smart. In her younger days, Patsy had seen him fight rats as big as cats and with one sniff avoid tasty looking puddles of antifreeze, one drop capable of killing painfully.

As Manny rowed, Patsy wondered why her friend had chosen to live with this crazy man. And did he know anything about Mimi's disappearance? She settled onto the wet wood, her tail an inch from Big Black's face, her paws clinging to the slippery deck as the river pushed and the ocean pulled them toward the Singing Bridge.

Love, she thought. Love.

"Big Black is old now," Manny said, stopping to take off his hospital robe, fold it neatly, and stuff it under his okole. "Woods tough on the butt." He looked over his shoulder and said, "If he was younger, he'd chase a fine-looking tanker like you." A thin line of blood reached from Manny's forehead to his chin. He brushed it away, but when he dug the oars into the water, the blood returned. "Girl like you reminds me of sunny days and summer storms."

As he guided the boat toward the bridge, his back muscles bulged, relaxed, and bulged again. Eyes still closed, Big Black swung his tail slowly back and forth.

"After you deliver your message, you can set sail with us if you want, but like I say, Big Black is old, and me, well, I only go where the Madonna tells me to go. You can't depend on me. Better you should try one of the inter-island tugs. Good food on tugs. Go to Honolulu. Maybe catch a ship from there. See the world.

"The cruise ships are good. Best food in the world if you have to be on a ship. Course, it means putting up with noisy passengers and a noisier crew. Bunch of land guys thinking they're sailors. Most of them never been sailors and never will be. Plenty of mice, you can bet. Scrambled eggs and toast every morning, blue cheese dressing on the floor every evening." Manny dropped the oars and stretched his arms in the air. "Course, you can't go anywhere until you tell Steamer what I told you. Ah, it feels good to be working and bleeding. Cleans out the system."

The boat drifted toward the bridge while he talked over his shoulder.

"If you're thinking roundtrip, you got to be careful. No place like home. You get lost out there, you'll never find your way home. Happened to me more than once."

Patsy watched a human walk to the middle of Singing Bridge and climb slowly over the railing.

Manny dipped one oar into the water, then the other, just enough to keep the boat straight in the current. "This is the place for you. You can't leave it. Buildings out there are taller than waterfalls, so tall they block out the sun."

As the bridge grew bigger, Patsy saw that the climber was a woman wearing a white bathing suit, the kind that the flat women wore in the black-and-white world. She was leaning out over the water with her hands behind her holding the bridge.

"You know Honolulu is built on a swamp? A big sinking stinking swamp. Best seen in moonlight when you can't see half the bad stuff. Alleys and lots of drain pipes. Streets filled with dogs. You wouldn't like it. Big Black will tell you."

Big Black continued his snoring.

"You could hold your own, sure. You're one Hilo girl, a big blue-eyed cruiser from the Palace. But you got a job to do." Manny dropped the oars and pointed up at the sky. "That's what she said."

Patsy looked up and saw a flash of feet, white suit, arms crossed, hair flying, and then a splash. The skiff rocked left and right. Manny's foot slipped, and he fell back, grabbing for the oars.

"Not again," he shouted.

Big Black continued snoring.

After pulling himself up, Manny shoved the oars into the skiff and leaned over the side, searching the dark water.

"There!" he shouted, and without standing up he launched himself over the side. Still stuck to his okole, the hospital gown launched with him, hit the water, and spread itself at the surface before sinking slowly in pursuit of its quickly descending owner.

Big Black yawned. The boat drifted under the bridge and toward the bay. As cars passed overhead, Patsy thought about jumping in, going to Manny's assistance. She was a good swimmer. The woman had taught her many techniques in the claw-foot tub at the Palace. But before she could jump in, Manny surfaced at back of the boat, sucking air and treading water. "You see anything?" Without waiting for an answer, he dropped back underwater.

Long fingers grabbed the bow and pulled Doc Trina's head above water. She tossed a plastic bag in the boat and held a finger to her lips. "Shhhhh."

Manny bobbed up at the back of the boat.

"I coulda swore I saw a white bathing suit down there," he said. "Old style, like Ester Williams wears in the movies. The Madonna is old style but not even she wears a big suit that old."

"People with taste do," Doc Trina said.

"That you talking, Patsy?"

Patsy heard splashing, felt the bow go up, and saw Manny pull himself over the stern. Behind him, two hands grabbed the soaked wood. They were delicate hands with long fingers.

"What a surprise," Manny said. "A doc who makes house calls."

"You think your suit is any better?" the Doc asked. She draped her arms over the back of the boat and pulled herself up. Her smooth skin glistened with drops of water.

Manny grabbed the oars and shook the water from his hair. A few drops landed on Patsy's fur. She licked them. They were salty and reminded her of tears.

"Where do you think you're going?" the Doc asked from the stern.

Manny dug the oars into the water and pulled hard and deep. "I'm going where I was going." His back muscles bulged.

"That makes sense," the Doc laughed. "Have you eaten yet?" She kicked her feet, pushing the boat like a kickboard.

"You don't want to be dangling back there too long," Manny said. The boat passed under the bridge. "We're in the ocean now. Plenty animals in here."

Looking over the side, Patsy saw coral heads, some of them green. Most of them were brown, dead from the river's fresh water.

"I'm not afraid of animals."

"Get in the boat or kick harder."

The Doc pulled herself half into the boat, head down and butt in the air while water rushed over the stern. "Patsy, what are you doing out here?"

A wave passed under the skiff, made it rise and fall as the water level rose to Manny's ankles.

"You don't want to be blamed for the deaths of these cats," Manny said. "Big Black he forgot how to swim years ago."

Big Black was asleep, and the palm trees along Bay Front were waving as two surfers paddled away from the beach, leaving behind three old men casting bamboo fishing poles.

Doc Trina flopped into the boat and sat in the pool of water. "What did you say about my bathing suit?" She dug into the cooler. "It's retro, that's what Papa Joe called it when he sold it to me. What do you call that thing you're wearing?"

"Minimal." He strained at the oars, pulling the boat through the surf while the Doc produced cotton swabs and a brown bottle. She soaked the swabs with liquid from the bottle and dabbed it on his bleeding knees and shoulder.

"You're a good sailor, Doc."

"You're a good bleeder."

"I look at a woman like you, I get thoughts."

"Quite a compliment."

Patsy saw a helicopter circle the bridge then head up river.

"They'll find you," the Doc said.

"Not before I set sail. They'll have their hands full with the two beer boys. Left the other one up river. Both of them could use a little fine tuning."

The Doc dabbed at Manny's thigh as a small wave carried a surfer toward town.

"I got some good tequila back at the boat," Manny said. "Why don't you help me drink it?"

Patsy saw the bandstand and the restaurant where Mimi sat with Teresa and drank tequila. They would drink glass after glass until their faces turned red and their voices grew louder and louder. Patsy remembered Teresa saying that tequila made her want to kiss people, and kissing people had caused her to produce three children with three different fathers. Patsy was not certain what this meant but more than once she had seen Teresa drinking tequila in the Empire, and she wondered if Papa Joe had a source of miniature humans hidden somewhere in his dusty books and cardboard boxes.

"Nice line," The Doc said.

"We'll sail together, past the horizon to a place I know. Only me. And live happily ever after."

"You're in no shape to live happily."

Two canoes headed toward the open ocean, six men in each, digging hard.

"I know," Manny said. "We're sinking."

The Doc used her hands to scoop water from the boat and slosh it back into the ocean. The water splashed on Big Black but it did not wake him.

Patsy heard his heart beating. Did he know the way to the secret place called happily ever after? Did Doc Trina? Was Mimi already there, waiting?

Love, Patsy thought. Love.

Doc Trina stopped bailing water and knelt in front of Manny. She leaned toward him, wrapped her arms around him, and kissed him on the lips.

Chapter 14

Papa Joe tried not to hear

sirens as he searched the first page of Johnny's letter
for the line where he had stopped reading.

> *Hey Joe,*
> *It's been a long time...*
> *Uncle, you kept me out of trouble...*
> *Back then I was working construction...*
> *Anyways, the owner of the club one night*
> *he needs someone to walk him out to the*
> *car because he's carrying money, so I go,*
> *and we're walking out to the car and a*
> *couple of punks they come...*

"Not finished with that letter?" Teresa asked.

"I'm working on it." Papa Joe gave up and turned the page. "This is one long letter."

> *Anyways, hell, I don't know where all that came from, maybe from all the movies I watched at the Palace but the owner he's impressed. He's standing there all smiles and he hands me a hundred dollar bill, and the next night he's buying me drinks and we get to talking. And he introduces me to one of the new girls.*
>
> *She's a hostess. Not one of the dancers. That's good, I guess, because some of those dancers are tough even without their clothes on. Her name is Antonia and she listens to him talk about the fight outside and he tells her to take care of me.*
>
> *From then on, when I come in to work, she brings me a drink and says hello and asks how I been then she goes back to her work which is being nice to the old guys. She's good with them, you know, acting like their friend. She doesn't have to take her clothes off, just be nice and act like she's glad to see them. Light their cigarettes and keep her hand on their knee. And laugh at their jokes*
>
> *Most times I don't like people that pretend they like someone just to make a some cash but after working there and meeting her, I got to thinking what I would*

*do if I needed money bad enough, and it
came down to pretty much anything
except hurting someone bad or lying to a
friend. And those old guys aren't really
her friends, they're just customers and
know they're getting only what they pay
for, if you know what I mean.*

*Anyway, Antonia, that's her name,
did I tell you? If you're reading this letter,
you've seen her and you know how good
looking she is so I'm not going to waste
any time describing her.*

*Plus, she's good at laughing without
being loud, and she knows how to smile
while still being serious, kinda respectful,
and she never cheats any of the old guys
on the bill, and she's always polite and
quick and gets whatever they need. She's
good at listening and tells them when it's
time for them to go home. She never wears
perfume so the old guys don't stink it up
when they go home, unless they want her
to wear perfume, because some of those
old guys got nobody to go home to and
they like to go to sleep smelling her.*

*She told me there are lots of men
like that and I got to thinking about
myself.*

*Anyway, after that, whenever I pass
her, I lean close to see if I can smell a tiny
bit of something interesting, and if I do I
know the guy she's with is one of those*

lonely guys and I think about being alone at night and smelling her perfume.

Even the girls like her. Some because they think she likes girls. You'd be surprised, there's a lot of those kind in the bar business. But Antonia has a nice way of saying no, so they don't get mad. They still act nice to her, which is good because some of those girls are tough.

Antonia's not high nose. After hours she hangs out with all of the girls for one drink, no more, and I get to thinking why only one? Sometimes we say a few things to each other, her kidding me about working too hard and we go to the movies. She likes the movies. And we have a few drinks.

After a while I get to thinking how good life could be if there wasn't something missing. I'm thinking that I could probably work double shifts until I was fifty or sixty and if I was real careful I could save up enough to maybe move to Oregon or Washington or someplace in Canada and buy a small piece of land, you know, a lot big enough for a house. For me and her.

I guess that kind of thinking can screw a guy up.

Then I look at Antonia. Then I think some more, and I get to thinking what it would be like to have a woman to come home to at night, maybe a woman who could smile and say nice things to me. You know?

Sure, there are plenty of women in Honolulu but for a guy working two jobs to save cash it's not easy to find a good one. If they got anything going, they look at me and see a guy with one pair of jeans and no car, sharing rent with two other guys. And if they're like me working a couple jobs and trying to pay rent, they don't have time to look at me.

I'm not the smartest guy, so I go to the owner and I ask him about Antonia, and he says, well, she's got a contract but maybe we can work something out. Maybe next time around, when he brings in some new girls I can get one of them but I tell him I'm set on Antonia, and he shakes his head and says more stuff about me waiting for the next group, and I got to thinking something was wrong.

So I go to Antonia and I tell her I want her, and she gets nervous and scared so now I know something is wrong.

I keep an eye on her, and make a point to drop in when I got extra time, just to see what she's doing. And I start seeing this guy with her. He's a local guy, a regular who I've seen before because he comes in a lot. He's a big guy and the other bartender tells me he's part of the syndicate but he says that about alot of guys. So I keep watching her and I see

*how the guy treats her, touching her all
the time and moving his hand up her leg
and the other girls tell me...*

Papa Joe rubbed his eyes. Looked at Teresa
and asked, "You ever meet one of those girls who
works in the hostess bars?"
"Plenty. What? You don't remember?"
Papa Joe went back to reading the letter.

*...he's in the syndicate so I figure
he's in the syndicate but by then I didn't
care. I know he's got ideas about Antonia,
and I got a big problem because now every
time I look at her with him, I feel like my
gut is going to rip open unless I kick his
ass.*
　　　　*Anyway, now I start planning how
much money I'll need to take care of her,
and where we should live and what I need
to do to get a decent job. I'm thinking of all
the paper work I'll have to do to get her
legal. I'm thinking I got responsibilities
and it makes me feel good. Plenty guys tell
me I should try the army because it's not
like the old days, I can make good money
and get more if I have a wife and maybe
get training so I can get a job when I get
out. Maybe go to school.*
　　　　*Okay, that part about school is
crazy. Forget that part. That won't
happen.*

Anyway, one night I'm sitting in the club waiting for Antonia to finish work and I go over to the owner, because I figure I owe him, and I tell him I'm taking Antonia and we're going to the mainland.

He just looks at me like he doesn't understand, so I say it again, and he tells me I'm crazy and to forget it, then asks me about her papers and what am I going to do about that? He's paying to keep her here. I tell him I'm still taking her with me but I'll work something out with him. So he says he's got business to do and we can talk later. I go out in the bar and drink for a couple hours while I keep an eye on Antonia, make sure she's okay.

I wait until she's finished working and she walks out with me and I tell her I want her to quit and get married, just dumping it all on her in one gulp, while we're walking and in the parking lot the club owner he's standing with a couple of guys I don't recognize, but I see the big guy in a BMW, watching.

The club owner he's all nervous like last time I seen him and he shouts at me to go back inside when one of the two guys grabs him and throws him against a car, not the Beamer. And the other guy slams him in the face hard and he slumps down on the asphalt. Its like they don't even see me and Antonia but she screams

*and then they come after me. I get hit
hard, the two guys work on me, you know.*

*I'm out. Black. Don't even get in a
punch. And when I wake up I'm in one of
the tourist hotels downtown, I've got some
bruises but no holes in me, and Antonia is
there with a kid, a boy. If you're reading
this letter you know who I'm talking about.*

*Antonia says the girls inside called
the cops and the guys hitting me drove off
when they heard sirens, and the girls got
us out of there.*

*We're in the hotel room, and the
boy's name is Anthony, not Tony. He's a
good kid, quiet and smart, she says. And
she tells me she has money stashed
away, she says they're looking for us.
That doesn't bother me because I can take
care of myself but she's worried because
she thinks they'll send her back and she
doesn't want the boy to go back. There's
nothing there for him.*

*That's when she tells me some old
story stuff you probably heard before. The
kid's father is in the army, a guy from the
mainland and they lived together until he
shipped out when Anthony was only a
couple years old. And she hasn't seen him
since. She keeps the kid away from the
bar so no one knows about him. And he
doesn't know about them so he can grow
up a regular kid.*

Anyway, that's what she tells me and I believe her.

The only thing I can tell you about the kid is he's kinda small for his age, but he's quiet and quick and speaks English better than me. Antonia says he's smart and listens to instructions. And he's not one of those high-nose kids too smart to be friends with other kids and he's good with his hands, even though like I said he's kinda small for his age.

Hey look. I know how tough it is to make money especially with a kid. What a woman does to get by is her business. You gotta do what you gotta do. Right?

I know you're thinking I'm just another dumb guy making a dumb mistake. I don't blame you. I was thinking the same thing, thinking I should run out fast as my legs will carry me. I mean a kid is a lot of responsibility. Then I'm looking at her and I want to sleep with her, and I'm wishing I was smart enough to say what I mean and be with her and her boy.

You know I'm not one of the quickest thinkers but Antonia is smart and we figure it'll be easier if we split up. I'll go straight to the mainland and she can hide out for a while on the Big Island until things quiet down.

That's where you come in.

lz

Chapter 15

"Ernesto."

Ernesto felt sturdy fingers lift him from sleep. As he opened one eye, he saw a stinky Tuna Tidbit roll off his stomach and fall toward the dresser drawer.

"Wake up," Antonia said, cradling him in her arms. "We've been looking all over for you."

Ernesto's front paws relaxed as she rocked him gently awake then back to sleep. He was proud of the fact that over the years he had mastered the technique of being awake while still being asleep.

Using this technique of half-sleeping he could keep track of everything happening in the waking world without losing a wink in the sleeping world. He had developed this skill because of his need to know everything that happened at the Palace while living with Patsy and Mimi, two girls who could remain active for days without closing their eyes.

While he half-slept, he let Antonia shift him to one arm while she tried to close the drawer. "You made a mess here. Does Steamer allow you to do this?" She rolled him onto the bed, and he watched her through tiny slits formed by well-trained eyelids. To add to the effect he purred loudly, the same method he used to draw Patsy from hiding during the chase game.

But the sight of Antonia picking up stray treats and carefully returning them to their plastic-bag prison made Ernesto nudge his eyelids open a tiny bit more. When she rolled up the plastic bag and set it on the windowsill, he felt his world grow and begin to glow. Lulled into a false sense of security by his half presence, she had failed to secure the seal on the plastic bag. One tap and the remaining tasty treats would spill onto the floor. From his soft spot on the bed, he could smell them calling out to him for rescue.

Antonia studied the picture on the nightstand, rubbed her finger over Steamer and Mimi and Papa Joe as they held their glasses high at Reuben's.

"She is a pretty woman," Antonia said.

Ernesto said nothing. He could smell Steamer in the air and a far away memory of the woman on the sheets. He imagined the two of them sitting on the bed, both pretending to listen to the rain on the tin roof, a trick each used to gain a good position for the start of a wrestling game.

He opened his eyes wider when he saw Antonia digging in the drawer. She found the letter, his underwear pillow, and Mimi's black beads. She held the beads up to the light and looked at the picture again.

Ernesto did not move, even though he wanted to tell her to put the beads back in Mimi's drawer because Mimi would need them when she returned. They were a present from Steamer, a present that Mimi used whenever she needed to kneel in the corner and talk to her friend in the rafters, the girl that she called Hail Mary.

"I wonder why she did not take it with her?" Antonia asked.

Ernesto stayed still. The most important part of half-sleeping was never being tricked into waking. He half-watched as Antonia kissed the rosary and set it on the dresser. She folded the socks neatly, placed them in the drawer, and picked up the letter. It had been torn in half and stuck together with duct tape. The woman rubbed her fingers over the return address.

"Do you know anything about this? It's from your government."

Ernesto had no government.

A dog barked.

Antonia walked to the window and held the envelope to the light. "Not good," she said, and set the letter on the sill, picked up the camcorder. "And this?"

She flipped open the small screen and pressed buttons the way Steamer did. Ernesto heard the whir of film rewinding. She pushed another button and he saw Mimi's face appear, trapped in the camera screen, shouting above the sound of fireworks, "*New Years. For my lover. From Mimi!*"

Mimi waved clouds of smoke away from her face. "My name is Mimi O'Toole, daughter of Francis O'Toole and Mary Sugai O'Toole, both deceased."

Ernesto hopped to his feet and stared at the tiny screen. Somehow, she had managed to escape from the prison of the flat people in the projector room and make her way to her favorite bedroom. She was in the camera now only inches away from him, but her voice sounded far away. Wearing her Matsunaga for Congress t-shirt, with her hair cut short and combed back, she was too small to be Mimi. Mimi was a giant person, capable of scaling the ladder stretched over the alley and vanishing into the darkest night. Capable of carry the old popcorn popper into the alley and tossing it next to the dumpster. Capable of pinning Steamer to this bed and holding him there until he admitted defeat.

This Mimi he saw now in the flat world had been reduced to almost nothing.

"Being of sound mind and body," Mimi said, "if anything should happen to me, all I own goes to Steamer. That's the name he's going by now. I don't know his parents or his real name, or if he has a real name but he lives in the Palace and he's a hard worker. And he's not as crazy as he acts."

Behind her, the sky exploded orange and red. Mimi held up a bottle of tequila, drank a quick shot, then spoke to the camera.

"And you, Steamer, no matter what happens, don't let them hook me up to a machine. I don't want anything to keep me breathing while I'm dead."

Ernesto could make no sense of these words but they filled him with dread, especially the words *hook* and *machine*. He had seen Steamer trapped in his computer chair and he had seen what the flat people on the big screen were capable of doing. Were these smaller flat people capable of greater crimes? Did they have an electric chair that killed and kept a person alive at the same time?

Firecrackers exploded. Mimi's face appeared. "Nothing is going to happen me," she said. "But if it does. Just burn me up and toss what's left into the ocean. That's where I want to end up. Not in the bay, with the dead pigs and the cruise ship crap. I want to be out in the ocean on the other side of the breakwater, in the clean water."

A bottle rocket streaked across the sky in the tiny screen. Then a huge bottle of tequila appeared, blocking Mimi's face, then dropping away. Mimi swallowed and said, "One last thing. Please, please, please, please fix the toilet! If I come back and that toilet is broken, I'll kill myself."

Antonia pressed a button and the screen went black. She picked up the letter and placed it carefully in the drawer, looped the rosary twice over her wrist so that it fit like a bracelet, and said, "For extra help." Then she carried the camera, with Mimi still trapped inside, out of the room.

After a moment of thinking, Ernesto followed her through the projection room, down the stairs, and around the corner to the men's room.

She stopped in front of the wall where the human's marked their territory by peeing on white porcelain. "Papa Joe is right," she said. "These are the biggest urinals I have ever seen."

Even though Ernesto did not understand the meaning of urinals, if Papa Joe had said it, the words must be true. He watched the woman turn to face the two stalls where the humans sat when they needed a quiet place to read and do their business behind closed doors. On the door to right, Steamer had duct-taped a sign: *Giggle the handle*!

Antonia laughed and set the video camera on the paper towel dispenser. She rolled the rosary bracelet off her wrist and dropped it carefully into her jeans pocket. Then she lifted the toilet seat. "This is not so bad," she said, "I have seen worse."

Ernesto hopped up to the sink. From there he could see the woman reaching for the knob on the toilet that was supposed to send dirty water whirling away and clean water pouring back in, a cycle the humans repeated often after watching the flat people. When Antonia pushed it, a pool of clear water spiraled down and out of the Palace. None returned.

"I see," she said.

Ernesto saw nothing. That was the problem. The water was gone and now it would not return. The woman lifted the heavy lid behind the seat and set it on the bowl. "Hmmm," she said, standing over the toilet, pushing and pulling at the toilet's insides. "Yuck."

Ernesto slipped into half sleep, dreaming of the rosary and ways to retrieve it, thinking that if the woman really wanted to watch water flow she should go to the river and the waterfall. Patsy had told him it was very beautiful there with tiny fish that could be scooped out with a single sweep of her paw.

And if the woman wanted to do other things, he could show her a spot in the alley, a nice patch of grass where she could do her business without wasting water in the process and the only danger would be the sudden appearance of the Bopper.

"There is always hope," Antonia said, pulling her hands out of the toilet and shaking them over the sink. She rubbed her hands with the green liquid, held them underwater, and dried them with a paper towel. Ernesto followed her up the stairs to the box office and watched her search through the drawers until she found a box of paperclips, strung three of them together, then hurried back to the men's room.

"This is an old trick," she said.

Ernesto jumped to the sink then to the paper towel dispenser, where he brushed off a stray clump of Patsy's fur and watched Antonia take off her shirt so she could hang it on the hook behind the door.

Ernesto was not surprised at this behavior. All humans, especially the flat ones, enjoyed taking off their clothes. He had seen it happen so many times on the flat screen that he wondered why they ever put clothes on, unless it was only so they could take them off. One time, Steamer had posted a picture on the box office window of two humans taking off their clothes, with a written promise that they would return at 7:30. The Palace had filled so quickly that Papa Joe could not find a seat and had to stand in the aisle for two hours as the two flat people chatted over dinner, walked in the woods, and held hands in the moonlight before someone in the audience yelled "Get to the good part!" and for once the flat people did what they were told, throwing off their clothes and engaging in a serious but somewhat hard to follow wrestling match that lasted only a few minutes before the credits rolled.

"There," Antonia said, pulling her hands out of the toilet. When she pushed the knob, the water made a noisy fuss while running away, waited a moment, and then made a noisy fuss returning to its original level. "Finished," Antonia said.

She washed her hands, dried them, and washed them again before pulling the shirt over her head and picking up the camera. "What do you have to say about that?" she asked. Before Ernesto could answer, she pressed a button on the camera. In the tiny screen, Mimi shouted, "Time to celebrate!"

Papa Joe appeared in the tiny street, tugging at a string of bright red firecrackers. "Fire in the hole!" he shouted and used a tiny lighter to set the fuse on fire. The flame jumped and hopped, sputtered, flashed back to life, hit the first cracker in a long line of crackers.

"Taiwan Bucket Blasters!" shouted Papa Joe as he backed away, covering his ears with his hands. First came a pop, then an explosion, bright and yellow, then one after the other, flashing cracks of exploding light, crawling up the line, a dragon of fire weaving its burning body from the sidewalk toward the top of the Palace's neon sign.

"Hold me," Mimi shouted. "Pray for peace."

The flashes climbed upward. The explosions grew louder. And Steamer appeared holding Mimi, their faces close to each other, lips touching.

Antonia pressed a button and snapped the camera shut. "Some things are private," she said to Ernesto. "Isn't that right?"

He followed the woman up the stairs and back to Mimi's room, keeping an eye on the camera, thinking that now he had many more problems. Steamer and Papa Joe were trapped in the camera with the woman. He watched her set the camera down on the windowsill.

"Pray for peace," she said.

Ernesto did not know how to pray. He watched her through eyelids squeezed almost shut as she shook out the sheets, smoothed them flat, and tucked them under the bed. Was that praying? She fluffed the pillows and covered the bed with Patsy's quilt, the thin one he liked for sleeping because Patsy had worn an extra-soft spot into its smooth cotton.

The woman looked around the room, shook her head, and knelt down next to the bed. She pressed her hands together and bowed her head, whispering something that Ernesto could not hear. Then she looked up at the rafters and in a soft voice said, "Hail Mary."

In his tiny head, Ernesto saw firecrackers explode.

Chapter 16

Steamer fingered the nylon collar in his pocket.

"Up here!" Mr. Goodmorning called.

Steamer jerked the backpack high on his shoulders and checked both ends of the street. It was just a street, empty except for Mimi riding a beach cruiser with balloon tires down the center, waving to him as she coasted toward the ocean.

"Wake up! Steamer!"

Steamer looked at the sky. It had turned dark blue, with thick clouds moving in from the ocean, with the smell of rain and the promise of danger. Mr. Goodmorning was up there in the rain clouds waving his thin arms.

That was good. In *CasaNoir*, the weather changed often and without warning. Its quick cuts and scenes spliced together from five different movies had made it almost impossible to avoid a few minor irregularities, such as the sudden appearance of a torrential downpour in the middle of what had been a sunny day. But since the action was set in Hilo, such lapses in continuity could be explained as realistic.

"Steamer."

"What?"

"He's up here."

"Who?"

Mr. Goodmorning pointed inside, cupped his hands over his mouth and tried to shout a whisper, "Your boy."

On the sidewalk in front of Mr. G's door, Steamer found an Oreo cookie. A fading *For Rent!* Sign was taped to the cracked wood. He pushed the sign, and the door swung open, revealing a narrow hallway that led up sagging stairs. The perfect location for a scene in *CasaNoir II*. He followed the sticky shag carpet up the stairs, past another Oreo, and when he reached the top he found two more cookies in front of a door painted flat black. A naked bulb hanging from a frayed cord heavy with dust and cobwebs provided the only light.

Steamer was about to knock, when the door swung open and Mr. Goodmorning stepped out. "No one following you?" he asked, checking the stairs. "Good."

Steamer smelled patchouli and river water.

"I'm worried about you," Mr. Goodmorning said, picking up the cookies and putting them in his pocket.

"I wouldn't eat those."

"Of course not." Mr. Goodmorning pulled him inside and slammed the door. "Cleaning up the trail. We'd better get the other ones on the way out. No, I guess the roaches will take care them. You're getting a little slow, Steamer."

Steamer stopped in the middle of a room. The boy was sitting there next to a pile of clothes spilling out of a wooden packing crate. There was no furniture, just floor space and a row of big windows with cloudy glass. He could almost see through them. When he squeezed the boy's shoulder, Anthony smiled.

"You have to wake up," Mr. Goodmorning said, tucking a white dress shirt into faded blue jeans. "This boy is quick, with some Patsy in him."

"I was standing in front of the Palace and I turned around and he was gone."

"He's quick," Mr. Goodmorning said. "You got to keep an eye on the quick ones. Who were those men?"

"Tourists."

"They didn't look like tourists. The boy took one look at them and ran."

"That's the only way to escape from tourists."

"Be nice," Mr. Goodmorning said. The wall facing the windows was lined with peeling mirrors and a brass bar for stretching. Mr. Goodmorning padded barefoot across the floor and leaned against the bar. Now that Steamer saw his neighbor full length instead of hanging out of a window, Mr. G looked lean and agile, lanky. His short hair and clean shave gave him a modern look, hip and updated.

The boy tossed Mr. G an Oreo cookie, high and wide, but he caught and popped it in his mouth in one quick motion. "I don't trust those guys," he said as he crunched.

"Me neither," Steamer said. He did not know what guys Mr. Goodmorning was talking about but he knew he had many things to do and trying to communicate with Mr. G was something he had always left to Mimi. He loosened his backpack straps and said, "I got a list of things to do."

"Sit here," Mr. Goodmorning said.

The three of them sat cross-legged on the floor while Steamer dug in his pack and handed Mr. Goodmorning a plastic container full of scrambled eggs. "Not as good as Mimi's but good," he whispered, hoping the boy did not hear him.

"Who made these?"

As Steamer pictured Mimi frying rice and eggs with sausages and green onions, the boy said, "My mother."

"Good. I won't eat Steamer's eggs. You should take my advice and avoid them. He's a heavy handed cook."

Steamer counted twelve packages of ramen, a bottle of Tapico hot sauce, two cans of Spam, and pushed the pile toward Mr. Goodmorning.

"My favorites," Mr. Goodmorning said.

"I'm doing Mimi's good deeds. Still got books to deliver to the jail. Fliers to post"

"And this boy?"

"He's a good boy."

"I know that. I can see that by looking at him. Where did he come from?"

While the two men looked at him, the boy inserted an earphone into his ear and left the other earphone dangling. Whispers of violins entered the room.

"That's a good way to listen to music," Mr. Goodmorning said. "You can hear music and what's going on around you at the same time. This boy is smart."

"Anthony," the boy said.

"You don't look like an Anthony."

"He's not a Tony."

"I can see that," Mr. Goodmorning said. "But he's not an Anthony. Didn't you see the way he ran into the street and saved Ernesto? He's like one superhero. Tell me, Superhero, is your mother as pretty close up as she is from afar?"

"What kind of question is that?" Steamer said. "You don't ask a boy that kine question."

"Okay, let me ask you then. Is his mother as pretty as she looks?"

The boy smiled.

"His mother is from Honolulu," Steamer said. "Related in some way to Papa Joe."

"This boy?" Mr. Goodmorning gave the boy a close look. "Related to Papa Joe? I don't think so. This boy going to be small."

Steamer stuck the dangling earphone into the boy's free ear. "Listen, you have to be careful how you talk in front of the boy. Boys got feelings."

"I can hear you," the boy said.

"He's honest, this boy. You got yourself a good boy."

The two men watched the boy sitting with his legs crossed, back straight, nibbling on a cookie. Steamer was surprised at how clean the apartment smelled. He had expected Mr. G to be stinky.

"I hear you got a movie tonight," Mr. G said. "What kine movie?

"An anti-war movie with no killing."

"Any action?"

"It's not an action movie."

"Jeez, you know what can make movies without action seem good?" Mr. G asked.

"Cowboys," the boy said.

"I like cowboys," Mr. G said.

"Tough to find cowboys who aren't killing somebody," Steamer said.

"Yes," Mr. G said. "They do tend to get carried away. Cowboys got minds of their own." He laughed. "You tell cowboys to calm down, next thing they're shooting somebody."

The boy nodded and handed Mr. G another cookie.

"Problematic," said Mr. G.

"Problowmatic," said the boy.

"The trustees are coming tonight," Steamer said. "They're worried about the Palace."

"The Palace supposed to have movies. Haven't seen a movie over there in weeks, maybe months. Can't remember."

"I'm working on it."

"What your movie needs is popcorn. No one cares about the movie as long as they have good popcorn. You can show lots of bad movies like you do at the Palace as long as you got good popcorn."

"Trustees don't like popcorn. Too much noise."

"And red dogs. You should sell plenty red dogs. People like red dogs."

"I like red dogs," the boy said.

The two men looked at the boy, he blinked and they looked back at each other.

"He's kinda like a cat," Mr. Goodmorning said. "Something small but powerful and fast."

"He's a boy."

"You let me come over tonight, I'll run that snack bar," Mr. G said. "See, I'm clean. Smell me again. I take a bath every day in the river. Every day it's not raining. When I was a kid I used to spend a lot of time around snack bars. Fresh steamed red dogs, that's what your movies are missing."

Steamer put two more cans of Spam on the floor. The bright blue cans looked like they belonged in a movie. They were red, gold, yellow and blue and too beautiful to contain jellied pig snouts and miscellaneous pork byproducts.

Mr. G stacked the Spam cans, smiled. "Spam is good."

"They're a sign of trouble in Paradise," said Steamer.

"I like Spam," Anthony said.

"Spam is evil," Steamer said.

Mr. G covered the boy's ears. "Don't scare him."

"He should know the truth."

"How can food be evil?"

"Patsy," the boy said and touched Steamer's elbow.

"He's right," Mr. G said. "Patsy likes Spam."

Steamer stood up. "No, she doesn't, but I have to find her. Have you seen her?"

"How many times do I have to tell you? I see everything that happens in this town." He looked at the boy. "Let me introduce myself."

The boy blinked.

"People around here call me Mr. G for short, but my real name is David Goodmorning. You're the only one who knows my first name, except for Mimi. The David part is real. She knows. And now Steamer knows, and you."

"Don't confuse the boy."

"Not me. I wouldn't do that. Except some time. Confusion is good. Lots of good things come from confusion."

Steamer gave him a close look. Mimi had seen something good in this man. Close up, he looked clean enough and he had the classic face for a leading-man role, athletic in a non-athletic way, healthy and full of energy. But Steamer had never seen him anywhere except hanging out his window.

"I'm invisible," Mr. G said.

The boy nodded and said, "I would like to be invisible."

"No, you would not," Steamer said. "How would your mother take care of you if you were invisible?"

"Don't scare the boy."

Steamer stood up and lifted the backpack onto his shoulders. "I have to find Patsy. Do you want to help us? Me and the boy?"

"As soon as I find my shoes." He dug through the pile of clothes until he found a pair of canvas reef walkers. "Left my slippers in my truck. Don't know why." He stood up and without putting on his shoes, took the boy's hand, and went out the door, saying, "Don't bother with the lock."

Steamer closed the door, tried to lock it, but gave up when the doorknob spun free in his hand. He followed the boy down the stairs and stood between him and Mr. G on the sidewalk.

"I seen Patsy head up to the Pink Church this morning," Mr. G said. "I'll bet she didn't stop there. Nothing much happens up that way."

An ambulance crossed in front of them, headed up the mountain. A police helicopter circled overhead. Sirens faded left and right.

Steamer thought of Mimi. He wondered about kids and people like David in a world with too many sirens.

"Exactly," Mr. G said. "We should go check the Humane Society. That cat Patsy always thinking about the past. Can't get it out of her head."

"How do you know that?" Steamer asked.

"It's obvious."

They headed toward the ocean, the boy and Mr. G walking in front. Mr. G pointed right and disappeared left, into the side of a building. Steamer ran to catch up and found a door not quite closed that he had never seen before. He pushed it open and peeked into the darkness. A hallway led to another door. The floor sagged under his weight. As he walked, Steamer wondered if every floor in Hilo sagged. He reached the door and it opened into a narrow ally. Mr. G and the boy were standing next an old red truck, something small and cramped with big tires and a smashed license plate.

"Truck doesn't run too good without Mimi," Mr. G said.

The boy patted the rusted metal of smashed fender. "Good truck."

"You got some Patsy in you," Mr. G said to the boy. He tossed his shoes in the back. "And Patsy she's got lots of Mimi in her so maybe you can help."

Steamer held the boy back. "Mr. G, are you a good driver?"

"Of course not."

"I have to keep this boy safe."

"You have to get out of that theater more often," Mr. G said. "That's what you have to do."

The boy nodded.

"Me and Mimi used to take this truck out to the freezing ponds to swim all the time," Mr. G said. "That's where we should take this boy someday so we can toughen him up for Hilo life. Stand out there and drink beer with the boys. Shoulders back, challenging the world. Saw Papa Joe out there once swimming with Teresa."

"This truck weighs a ton," the boy said.

"Heavy, sure, and a little bit picky when it comes to starting," Mr. G said, pulling open the passenger door. "Me first," he said. "The driver's side doesn't open."

"You have a license?" Steamer asked.

"Two of them."

Mr. G crawled across the seat, and the boy climbed in after him. Steamer hesitated. Then he slipped the pack off his shoulders and jammed it under the seat. After he squeezed in and closed the door, he felt as if he were on an inter-island flight, waiting to take off with his knees pressed against the seat in front of him and his head bumping the luggage rack.

"Cross your fingers," Mr. Goodmorning said. He pumped the gas and pulled the ignition switch but nothing happened. "Four cylinder," he said. "Takes a little maneuvering. Give it a pat, Anthony. There, above the radio. Doesn't like going anywhere without Mimi."

The boy rubbed the dash, patted the radio, and said, "Good truck. Good truck."

"Extra good." Mr. Goodmorning pulled the ignition but still nothing happened. "Anthony, try kicking the tires. That helps, sometimes."

The boy climbed over Steamer's lap, opened the door, and jumped down to the ground. He kicked the front tire twice. When Mr. G pulled the ignition, the engine sputtered to life. Exhaust fumes filled the alley as the boy climbed into the cab.

Steamer adjusted the side mirror. "What about those?" he said, pointing at the rubbish cans blocking their exit. "I'll move them," he said.

"Never mind," said Mr. G.

"Never mind," the boy said, plugging in both his earphones.

Mr. G stepped on the gas. He missed the first rubbish can, clipped the second one, and smashed the third one under the truck, dragging it two blocks before spitting it out in front of Reuben's Mexican Cantina.

Through the side mirror, Steamer watched the truck spewing a trail of blue smoke as it headed out of town.

Chapter 17

Patsy jumped ashore as soon

as the skiff touched ground at Coconut Island. She ran over the concrete footbridge to Queen Liliuokalani Park, ignored the fish in the tide pools, and didn't stop until she reached the hood of a black SUV. It was parked next to the Suisan docks. Inside were two policemen eating plate lunches from Styrofoam containers.

"That's a cat on the hood," the driver said, lifting up a forkful of rice and chili.

"Looks like a cat," said the passenger, using chopsticks to peel off a chunk of Korean chicken.

"Patsy from over at the Palace."

"Heard plenty things about that cat."

They nodded and chewed while they watched Manny's Malaysian junk bob at the dock.

"Friggin Manny Matos," said the driver.

"This time we got him."

"Gone too far, that Manny friggin Matos."

The driver mixed a scoop of rice into a wad of macaroni salad, then stink-eyed the junk. "When I see that friggin…"

"Manny Matos…"

"…I don't know what I'll do."

Behind them, still without any clothes, Manny dragged the boat onto the coral beach, crossed the footbridge, and waved to a group of tourists in front of the hotel. He jumped down to a patchy stretch of beach and tide pools, where he could move unseen toward the two men in the police SUV. Big Black walked a parallel course on the sidewalk.

"One thing about Manny," said the driver cop, "he's good for plenty overtime."

"Can't beat that."

"Gotta give em credit."

"Good football player at St. Joe's."

"I remember."

Keeping an eye on Patsy, the policemen chewed and nodded and remembered the old days at Hilo High. Those were good days except for having to sit in English and math class. The rest was good.

Patsy watched Big Black stop under a table at Uncle Cole's Plate Lunch Heaven for a stray chunk of seared ahi and a clump of white rice before he ducked under the cops' SUV, walked the dock, and jumped aboard Manny's Junk.

"Another cat," the driver said.

"I seen that cat before."

"Manny's cat."

"Old that cat."

Frying-fish fumes stoked by Uncle Cole and his three helpers drifted through the afternoon air. They teased Patsy's nose as she jumped from the SUV and landed on the sidewalk. If the woman was hiding in Manny's boat, Patsy would find her. She ran across the dock and leaped aboard the 40-foot junk. She sniffed the door to the cabin, searching for a way inside. The woman had been here. Patsy could smell her memory almost hidden beneath the strong smell of rotting canvas, waterlogged wood, and something sweet, something like cookies.

While Big Black settled into a curl at the bow, Patsy navigated the narrow spaces between the packing crates piled high on the deck and bulging at their duct-taped seams. She checked the main hatch and found it locked. She turned left, right, and ran by a rusty beach cruiser with its balloon tires flat, its chain sagging. Behind a greasy moped and a wounded surfboard, she found a porthole clean enough for her to peek inside the cabin. Boxes of Girl Scout cookies were piled on the galley table and scattered on the bunks. Charts were taped to the walls and two coffee cups were bobbing in the sink, but there was no sign of the woman.

Big Black yawned.

The boat reminded Patsy of Papa Joe's store. Both places were good for sleeping, rich with strong smells and comfortable cubbyholes. Both had plenty mice and tequila. But there was a difference. When she went to sleep at Papa Joe's, she knew that she could wake up days later and still be in the Empire. If she fell asleep here on *The Manila Queen*, there was no telling where she would wake up.

Big Black snored peacefully.

From atop the stern cabin, Patsy surveyed the docks. Manny was hiding behind Uncle Cole's army of rubbish cans. Her chase game experience told her that if he wanted to avoid the policemen, he would have to hide there until dark. By then the policemen would be heavy with sleep from eating like Ernesto. She blinked, looked again at the rubbish cans, and saw Rusty appear. Carrying something in his mouth, he ran to the middle of the street, stopped to glance back at Manny, and then hurried off toward the park, four tiny legs and a tiny tail hanging from his mouth.

Patsy looked from the quickly disappearing Rusty to the hiding Manny. Did he have the patience needed? Unlike Big Black and Papa Joe, who had fully developed sitting skills and were capable of remaining immobile for endless hours, Manny was a buzz-head, incapable of sitting in one place for more than a few seconds. If Patsy left now to catch Rusty, she might return to find Manny's boat gone and with it any chance to find Mimi.

There were many factors to be considered. She remembered the kitten's tiny mouth. It's tightly closed eyes. It was a small kitten, and Mimi was a big girl. The policemen had their clothes on, and Manny was naked.

Convinced that Mimi would agree with her decision, Patsy ran to the ladder and jumped. She checked the street for cars then crossed over, to the statue of Buddha. From there she could see the seventh hole of the golf course and the bamboo forest. A stray golf ball bounced onto the grass, hit a lava rock and ricocheted over Rusty's head. Without flinching, he kept moving, heading in the direction of the Ice House and the freezing ponds. Patsy was surprised that a dumpster diver who had come all this way while carrying a kitten was still capable of traveling so fast. If she was going to catch him before nightfall, she would have to devise a plan.

Seeking advice, she looked up at Buddha, but he remained silent in his concrete Zen. The sun was setting. She ran after Rusty, crossed a bridge over a school of fat red-and-white koi, to another bridge that led to a tall man using a bamboo pole to tap the branches of a flower tree, sending clouds of purple and yellow flowers into the air, falling like confetti on his jumping children.

In the fading light, Patsy saw Rusty drop the kitten dangerously close to a koi pond. From the driving range, a golf ball shot into the air, curved around the Nixon Banyan tree, skimmed over the bamboo forest, and struck the ground an inch from the kitten before it rolled into the pond.

Rusty picked up the kitten and ran.

Patsy followed. After spending half the long day on Manny's skiff, she enjoyed shuffling through the fallen bamboo leaves, thick and slippery, and running past children tossing a red beach ball. As she dodged through a wedding-party forest of legs, she inhaled the thick smoky taste of barbeque beef and teriyaki chicken. She smelled women in white gowns and men in black suits, ginger perfume and spicy aftershave, beer and pakalolo, and the sweet milky smell of Angelica's kitten.

Rusty shoved his way into a wall of bamboo.

Now Patsy had a chance. While he struggled through the thick bamboo, she would attempt the little-known short cut through the Ice House. That meant dealing with dogs and ghosts but she was not afraid.

Tail in the air, she ran through radio noise and children's laughter until she reached a chain-link fence. On the other side, two Dobermans paced up and down a narrow stretch of weedy grass. Beyond them, and on the other side of another fence, two Pit Bulls were chained to the loading dock. The smaller one tugged at its chain, the bigger one sniffed the air. At the entrance to the driveway, a hefty poi dog, a bizarre mix of Dobie, Pit Bull and Ridgeback, with a dirty white spot between its eyes, sat scratching its gnarly chewed-up ear.

If she could slip by the two Dobermans and between the Pit Bulls she could dive under the Ice House and escape out the other side. From there, she could make a dash for the freezing ponds, without having to deal with the ear chewer and with a good chance of catching Rusty as he came out of the bamboo.

Patsy remembered Papa Joe telling stories about the Ice House. Her favorite was the short one about Steamer working there as a security guard on the graveyard shift. Papa Joe always started the story by explaining how he had tried to warn him and how Steamer had insisted that he needed money to repair the orchestra pit. Besides, Steamer did not believe in ghosts, even if most people in town, including Mimi, considered them official ghosts left over from the great tsunami.

When Papa Joe was at the Palace, he always ended the story by pointing at the orchestra pit still in need of repair and saying in a deep voice, "One night. That's how long Steamer lasted. He's never gone back. Won't say why. But I tell you, I know money is not worth seeing what he saw. Not all the money in the world."

Patsy was not sure if she believed in ghosts but she knew she believed in Dobermans, and she did not like them.

Staying low, she dug at the ground under the chain-link fence while the Dobermans paced. She waited and watched. When the Dobermans split in opposite directions, she forced her head under the fence. As she pulled herself through, she scraped her back on a nasty piece of chain link. The Dobermans stopped, raised their noses, and caught her scent. When they saw her, they charged directly at her, like vice grips closing, but Patsy had already been running. She reached the next line of fence and burrowed her way underneath it as the Dobermans dropped their shoulders, dove at the white tip of her tail, and missed.

As the Dobermans crashed into the fence, she ran for the Ice House. Two Pit Bulls were waiting. They dragged their chains, slobbered and howled. They thrust their snouts into the air, snapping and growling. None of this bothered Patsy. Dogs always made noise. Too much noise. What was a little more barking? She zigged and zagged, throwing them off balance, then shot directly at them As they reached for her with sharp teeth and ragged nails, Patsy braked, jumped into the air, and sailed over the bigger dog, slashing her claws across his face before she landed on the back of the smaller Pit Bull. It twisted and snapped, and bucked Patsy to the asphalt. The Pit Bulls struggled to turn, slipped, and slipped again as the poi dog with the mangled ear lumbered up the driveway, moving a second too slow to catch Patsy before she disappeared under the Ice House.

In the crawl space under the rusty building, Patsy stopped to breathe. Dogs everywhere, not just the ones guarding the Ice House, were barking. In the park, in passing trucks, and in boats they voiced their discontent. At what, they weren't certain. But they had heard other dogs so they knew they should be barking. Big and small, fat and thin, they howled. Patsy didn't care. Their barking didn't matter. Dogs always barked in Hilo. The only thing that mattered now was the kitten in Rusty's mouth and the setting sun that would make it more difficult to find him.

Without thinking about ghosts, she followed a bulbous rat through the darkness. She thought of asking this rat if it was true that ghosts lived in the Ice House, but it was a fast rat winding its way through a maze of rocks, bricks and rusted rat traps at a remarkable speed, so she did not have time for asking questions. Before Patsy could even say hello, the rat popped out of the darkness into the fading light and ran across the grass to the freezing ponds. Patsy ran after it, and almost caught its tail before it dove into the pond. She watched it swim across water cold enough to turn Papa Joe's skin blue, and told herself that it was her duty to chase this quick fat rat. But it had helped her to escape and she had more important things to do. The sun was sinking.

When she turned away from the temptation, she saw Rusty, with the kitten still in his mouth, crawl out of the bamboo.

Chapter 18

Papa Joe stopped at the

canoe-club bulletin board. With Teresa's help, he had left a trail of movie posters and missing-cat flyers from Reuben's to this spot near the small-boat harbor. Behind them, all along the Bay Front playing fields, adults with beer bellies and knee braces threw themselves at each other in a slow motion game of football while spectators peeled missing-cat flyers from under their windshield wipers.

As Teresa surveyed the bulletin board, Papa Joe watched a six-man outrigger canoe make its way toward the mouth of the harbor, toward the open ocean and blue sky fading into nightfall. He smelled suntan lotion and diesel fuel and heard Doc Trina say, "Hey, Papa Joe!"

Rubbing a beach towel through her hair, the Doc stepped out from behind the King Kamehameha Canoe Club hale and stopped at the bulletin board. "You hear anything about a movie tonight at the Palace?" she asked.

"Movie tonight," Papa Joe said, "7:30, like always."

Doc Trina rubbed the towel under her arms. "Like always?"

Papa Joe figured that the almost never-used bathing suit he had sold her made her look about 115 maybe 125 pounds. "That suit going to last you a long time," he said. "Ester Williams model."

"Gets me lots of compliments."

"Really?" Teresa shook her head and handed the Doc a flyer. "You seen this cat?"

"That's a stick figure drawing."

"Steamer's not too good at drawing," Teresa said. "Supposed to be Patsy from the Palace."

"That doesn't look like Patsy."

"Big girl," said Papa Joe. "Ten maybe fifteen pounds."

"Spooky eyes," said Teresa.

"Cross-eyed," said the Doc. "I know Patsy. What's the matter with you guys? It's me, Doc Trina. You been drinking?"

"Been reading a letter."

"Been working."

Teresa covered three race announcements with a movie poster and held it there while Papa Joe applied liberal amounts of duct tape to each corner. Doc Trina rubbed her hair until it stood on end.

"Hair goes with the suit," Teresa said.

Hands on hips, Doc Trina examined the movie poster. "What's playing tonight? I can't tell from this poster. Is it Casablanca or Whale Rider?"

"That's a good question," Papa Joe said. "Can't understand Steamer when he starts talking about movies. Too much college in him. What you been doing?"

"Swimming."

"In the harbor?" Teresa asked. "No good to be swimming in that harbor."

The Doc rubbed her ears with the towel. "Nothing wrong with this water. It looks dirty but it's clean."

"Looks like something been chewing on your neck," Teresa said. "That happen while you were swimming?"

"Never mind that," the Doc said, draping the towel around her neck and shoulders. "How's that Steamer been doing?"

"He's surviving. Got him taking care of my boy's girlfriend and son."

"Your boy?"

"Johnny. He's kinda my boy, and the girl she's more than a girlfriend, in a way."

"Steamer's taking care of them?"

"I figure he's trying."

"Maybe you should tell him to come see me at the hospital."

"Hospital can't help Steamer," Papa Joe said, touching the letter in his pocket.

"You help Manny at the hospital?" Teresa said.

"What?"

179

"Cops said Manny escaped from the hospital. Said he stole a bunch of Girl Scout cookies." Teresa pointed a finger-gun at Doc Trina. "Girl Scouts can get mean about their cookies."

"Manny didn't steal any cookies," the Doc said. "He got in a fight, that's all. In Pearl City."

"Plenty people get in fights in Pearl City," Papa Joe said.

"Floated in the ocean for a few days," the Doc said. "Ate a few cookies. Saw a Golden Madonna."

"What kine Madonna?" Papa Joe asked.

"Golden. Says she saved him. Told him to eat the cookies so he could get back to Hilo and give Steamer a message."

"Said that?" Teresa asked.

"That and some other stuff that didn't make sense."

"I need to talk to Manny," Papa Joe said. "You know where he is?"

"Can you keep a secret?"

"No."

"Me neithers," said Teresa. "Not good with secrets."

Doc Trina wrapped the towel around her waist. "Then I can't say anything more about Manny." The towel was striped red, white and blue and made her look like she was wearing a flag. "But you better hurry if you want to see him. Last I heard he was catching the tide at midnight."

"What about the message?" Papa Joe asked.

"Said he gave it to Patsy."

Teresa pointed at the poster. "This one, the one in the movie?"

"Not that stick thing. The real Patsy, the kinda crazy, cross-eyed Patsy from the Palace." The Doc started walking toward town, shouting over her shoulder. "I can't tell you anything more, except you should hurry. You check Manny's boat. Bet you'll find Patsy. Or try the Second to Last Call. I'm going to check on Steamer."

The Doc was a fast walker. By the time Papa Joe figured out what he wanted to ask her, she was already out of shouting range.

"Strange, that Doc," Teresa said.

"She's like us. Not good with secrets."

"Where's her clothes?"

Papa Joe shrugged. He was wondering about the Golden Madonna and Manny's sailing skills. Under the red glow of streetlights blinking to life, he walked with Teresa along the main road and thought about storms at sea. They climbed the harbor bridge, stopped in the middle, and looked down at Manny's junk.

Teresa crossed herself.

"What's that for?" Papa Joe asked.

"For anybody who gets on that boat."

"You think crossing will help?"

"Can't hurt."

"Me, I'm old," Papa Joe said, "and I never seen crossing work."

A fishing boat appeared from under the bridge and headed into the bay while three men drinking beer huddled on the bridge.

Teresa said something about how many service guys she had seen get drunk and make the sign of the cross and go off to war and come back safe. "Remember this," she said. "There are no atheists in foxholes."

"Atheists must be smart. Good to stay out of foxholes."

The *Manila Queen* rocked gently in the fishing boat's wake, a wake that now included an aluminum beer can sinking. In the fading light Papa Joe saw Big Black asleep in the bow. "No Patsy," he said. "No Steamer."

"Just two cops," Teresa said.

"Where?"

"Over there. By Suisan. See the black car with the back open."

"Lots of black cars today."

They stood together, Papa Joe thinking that he liked living on boats but he didn't like sailing. He had spent too many years at sea. He would like to haul a boat like Manny's out of the water and plant it in the empty lot next to the Empire. Like Ernesto, he liked sleeping in tight places. He could sleep in the junk, and the girl and the boy could sleep in the Empire. The thought of her made him remember that she wore a cross and she looked like a Madonna.

"I hear Manny he get one head injury in the war," Teresa said.

"What war?"

"The war they had in his time. Everybody got some kind of war. He get one scar where the VD tore a hole in him."

"VC," said Papa Joe. "Manny, he's too young to fight VC."

Teresa kicked the "NO JUMPING" sign and asked, "Why build a bridge if you don't want anyone jumping from it?"

Papa Joe thought long and hard and waited for insights, especially insights about women and men and telling the truth. After running into a dead end at truth and circling back to sleeping on boats, he said, "I figure Manny's junk must weigh a couple of tons."

"At least," Teresa said. "Tough boat to save. His Madonna must be strong."

The air tasted of a dry storm. Somewhere the clouds were forming.

"Cops waking up," Teresa said.

They were big cops, heavy and slow, getting out of their SUV, pointing at the bridge. One of them yelled, "Hey you, no jumping!"

The other shouted, "No jumping."

Papa Joe waited for a hole in the traffic. "Now!" he shouted, grabbing Teresa's hand. They ran across four lanes of asphalt, both of them breathing hard by the time they reached the other side.

"Why we running?" Teresa asked.

"Don't know. Tired of walking."

The entrance to the Second To Last Call was behind the Iron Works building, in a shadowy corner facing the small-boat ramp. Papa Joe opened the door and stepped into a blue-light haze. He knew the place. Two rows of booths flanked a pool table and a karaoke machine. The booths on the left had a view of the loading dock, the ones on the right a view of corrugated iron but they were closer to the bar. The karaoke machine was broken. A door in the back led to a broken toilet and a busted window. A window big enough to crawl through.

"Close the door" the bartender shouted.

"Anybody seen Patsy?" Teresa asked.

"He went home hours ago," the bartender shouted.

"He's a she," Teresa shouted.

"Patsy? You mean Mimi's cat?" a familiar voice shouted from the shadows.

Papa Joe walked by ten wide-bodies lined up at the bar and found Manny in the last booth. He was wearing yellow rain gear with a HPD patch on the sleeve and playing a crossword puzzle by penlight.

Papa Joe squeezed in next to him so he could keep an eye on the bar, and Teresa took the empty seat on the opposite side of the table. She spread the last movie poster on the sticky table and asked, "You expecting rain?"

"Round midnight. Staying low," Manny said. "Not supposed to be hanging out in bars."

"You seen Patsy?" Papa Joe pointed at the stick drawing on the poster.

"That don't look like Patsy."

"That's what your friend Doc Trina said." Teresa poked her finger into Manny's chest. "Heard you ate all the Girl Scouts' cookies?"

"Had to. I've been converted."

"What kind of converted?" Papa Joe asked.

Manny told them the story about him being lost in a storm and the Golden Madonna appearing from the sea as a beautiful mermaid and telling him to live on Girl Scout cookies because she had a job for him to do."

"A Golden Madonna?"

"With Duct tape. Said she had been in an accident."

"War wounds," Teresa said, looking at Papa Joe. "Didn't I tell you?"

"What kine job?"

"Said to come back here and tell Steamer not to worry about Mimi, that everything was going to be okay."

"You done that?"

"Lots of interruptions. But I told Patsy. She can pass the word. Last time I seen her she was down by the Ice House playing with a couple of Dobermans."

Two cops came in, sat down at the curve in the bar, and ordered two shots of Yukon Jack and two beers. One of the cops got up and put a dollar in the karaoke machine. Nothing happened. He kicked it. The 102-inch TV lit up with dancing girls and the lyrics for "Witchy Woman" but no sound came out.

The waitress set three beers and three shots of tequila in front of Manny.

A dog barked.

"We got company," Papa Joe said.

They gulped their tequila, chased it with beer.

"Kinda slow in here today," Teresa said.

"Too slow in here for thinking," said Papa Joe, watching the cops glance in their direction.

"What kine thinking?" Manny asked.

"Been thinking about bar girls."

"Bar girls? What from WW Two?"

"A hostess."

"In a strip bar?"

"In a club," Papa Joe said. "You like those kine girls?"

"When women are taking their clothes off, it's hard not to like them."

They finished their beers and Manny shouted for another round. The cops looked at Papa Joe.

"This one doesn't take her clothes off," Papa Joe said. "Just brings drinks and sits with you and says nice things while she keeps her hand on your leg."

"Kinda hard not to like a girl that friendly," Manny said.

"She's getting paid to be friendly," Teresa said.

"Like I get paid for fishing and you get paid for feeding people?"

"We provide services to our customers and community. What service do strippers contribute?"

"Strippers perform a service," Manny said.

"A hostess, not a stripper."

"Believe me," Manny said. "You work all night doing it and don't get off until four in the morning after breathing cigarette smoke all night, you're doing a service. Sometimes the air-conditioning so high in those places, girls get pneumonia."

"Keep their clothes on they wouldn't get so cold," Teresa said,

"This girl keeps her clothes on."

"Not very friendly of her," Manny said.

The cops stood up. One wiped his mouth with the back of his hand. The other tightened his belt.

"You ever trust one of those girls?" Papa Joe said. "The illegal ones."

"Illegal to be a stripper?"

"She's from out of country."

"That's illegal? I know plenty girls from out of country. Nothing illegal about them. Knew one who married a professor up at the college. Took care of him after the car wreck."

"What car wreck?"

"It's long story."

Papa Joe spread the letter on the table. "I been wondering about that Golden Madonna of yours. The one with the duct tape."

The two cops pushed their way through the pool players and the extra-wide bodies sitting at the bar, then jammed themselves into the booth next to Teresa.

"What?" Teresa said, pushing back hard so that one cop had to sit with okole half-hanging off the seat. "This the only way you can get a date?"

"You stay out of this," the hanging-off cop said, standing up and bumping a pool player into a guy at the bar. "We've been looking for you, Manny."

"You, Matos. We've been looking."

Papa Joe saw it happen in slow motion, in steps like in one of Steamer's movies. The guy at the bar threw the pool player back at the cop. The thrown cop fell back against the sitting cop, who knocked into Teresa, and Teresa shoved back, splitting the cops in two. One of them caromed off the karaoke machine, the other one struggled to stay on his feet ,then hit the floor, hard, with his butt. The lights flickered, blacked out and sparked back to life as two beer-spattered speakers above the bar blasted out a screechy rendition of "Witchy Woman" and the cop managed to pick himself off the floor and fall back into Teresa's lap.

Then Teresa threw the first punch.

Chapter 19

E rnesto sat at the box office desk
and watched the woman unhook the top
button of her jeans. He kept his eyes on her. He had
already lost one woman and he did not want to lose
another. She still had Mimi's rosary in her pocket,
but her hands were soft, she knew how to fix toilets,
and she was good at distributing treats. In the
absence of Mimi, what more could a cat ask for?

She sat at Steamer's desk, picked up his pen,
and wrote blue words on white paper until someone
knocked three times on the door to the Palace and a
woman's voice shouted, "Open up!"

Ernesto hid under the desk while Antonia hurried to the door. Like Mimi and Patsy, she was a brave female. In Ernesto's experience, running away from noise produced better results than running toward it.

"Open up, Steamer. I know you're in there."

Two loud knocks shook the lobby.

"Steamer is not here," Antonia said.

"It's Doc Trina. Open up."

Ernesto rushed to Antonia and rubbed against her ankle until she unlocked the door. As door opened, fading light framed Doc Trina with her fist raised, ready to knock.

"I'm looking for the Steamer," she said and dropped her hand to help adjust the knot in the beach towel wrapped around her waist.

Ernesto rubbed his body against the rough cotton. He knew this woman. She was a good eater and knew how to share by holding food under the table when Mimi wasn't looking.

"He will be back soon," Antonia said, still blocking the doorway.

"Soon?" The Doc brushed the towel flat while looking past Antonia.

"He said that he would return to prepare for the movie. It starts at 7:30."

The Doc leaned down and rubbed behind Ernesto's ears. "Hello there, you little devil. What kine trouble you getting into?" The Doc straightened up and held out the same hand to Antonia. "You must be...?"

Ernesto watched the muscles in their arms bulge as the two women squeezed hands. Antonia was smaller than the Doc but held her ground without hissing or scratching or arching her back.

"My name is Antonia."

"Nice name. I just got through talking to Joe down at the beach. He didn't tell me anything about a woman staying here."

The Doc released her hand and looked around the lobby. "So you're looking after him? Alone?"

"He is looking after us."

"Well, yes, sure, he's that kind of guy. Hasn't been the same these days. Lacks focus, if you know what I mean?"

"I am not certain what you mean."

"Any chance the snack bar is open? I'm starving."

A moment later, Ernesto was sitting at the table in the snack bar, watching the Doc cut through a slice of ham that was surrounded by two scoops of rice and a pile of macaroni salad. Antonia placed the rice cooker on the table within easy reach. These two women did not take half measures when it came to food. The Doc forked in ham, brushed hair off her forehead, and used a clean paper towel to dab ham juice off her chin, all the while still chewing. She would have made a good cat. She knew the importance of eating and staying clean.

The Doc swallowed, wiped her mouth and said, "It's been a long day. You ever have one of those days?" Without waiting for an answer, she dug her fork into the rice. "I mean good days but with lots of strange problems."

Antonia nodded, sat down across from the Doc, and brushed a crumb off the table.

"I'm checking on Steamer, then I'm out." The Doc finished off the rice, jabbed her fork into the ham. "Steamer's coming back, right?"

"He promised to return."

"For the movie, right? If there is a movie." The Doc pressed her knife into the ham, and the ham fought back, refusing to be split in two. Ernesto would have taught it a lesson by biting it and tearing it into bite-size pieces.

"Steamer said there would be a movie."

The Doc chewed as Antonia poured her a hot cup of tea.

"Thanks. I've been meaning to switch to tea," the Doc said, picking up her cup. "Trying to stay off the caffeine."

Ernesto liked the way the Doc forked in more rice and gulped more tea even though Antonia was watching her closely.

"That's a pretty swimsuit."

"I get lots of compliments. You an old friend of Steamer?"

"Excuse me," Antonia said, getting up from the table. "I will be back in a moment."

Doc Trina reached for the teapot and in the process her hand brushed against Ernesto's cheek. The Doc had warm skin, like Antonia and Mimi had. She dropped a piece of ham in front of him. "Be careful," she whispered. "It's tough. The way you like it. Right, Ernesto?"

Before she finished speaking, he was already chewing through the salty meat and thinking that this was the way a cat was meant to live. The more women, the better, as far as he was concerned.

Antonia returned with a pair of rubber slippers. "You should not walk in bare feet. Steamer is still building and there are sharp things on the floor."

"Thanks." Between bites of food, the Doc slid her feet into the slippers. "I hope these aren't Mimi's. You know Mimi, right?"

"They're from lost and found. There are many pairs."

"Steamer used to put too much butter in the popcorn."

"I do not understand."

"Drip butter, mix in a coke spill and you get paste. Easy to get stuck in that. Before Mimi got rid of the butter, I had to abandon a couple pairs of sandals in here. Got up from my seat and walked right out of them. These might be mine. You did a nice job of cleaning them up."

Ernesto liked the paste made from sodas and sticky butter.

"This is mine," Antonia said, handing her a clean t-shirt. "You look cold."

"Thanks again." The Doc put down her fork and pulled the shirt over her frizzy hair. It was a tight fit and she had to wiggle to get it over her shoulders and to her waist. "My clothes were down by the bridge, left them too close to the water, got carried away by the tide." Now the Doc had *Club Fem Nu* written in black letters across her pink chest. "Thought I'd check on Steamer before going back to the hospital."

"Steamer appears to be healthy."

They looked at each other, and Ernesto recognized the situation. If they were cats, polite cats, they would have looked away, glanced back at different times so their eyes did not meet. These two were not polite. They stared at each other until the Doc said, "Appears?"

"I would like to ask for your help," Antonia said.

"Go ahead."

"When you are through eating."

Ernesto watched Doc Trina cut a piece of breakfast sausage with the side of her fork. Where had it come from? Why hadn't he seen it hidden behind the small pile of macaroni-potato salad? The Doc impressed Ernesto by finishing off the sausage and salad in two quick bites. She wiped her mouth with a napkin and said, "Ask away."

"There is a man who lives in the alley."

"Plenty of those."

"This one has a bat."

"The Bopper? Big guy? Weather beaten?"

"He is here now. In the alley."

"Show me." Doc Trina stood up first, and the two women left the table. Ernesto followed them to the back of the theater and out the door. The Bopper was sitting behind a pile of boxes, reading a Smart Shopper newspaper. His fingers poked out from behind thick white bandages.

"Plenty bargains in here," he said.

"Yeah, people supposed to get that in their mailboxes," Doc Trina said. "If they still have mailboxes after you get through with them."

A police car passed in the street, and Ernesto ducked behind a stray cardboard box. He had seen enough cars for one day.

"I'll do it," the Bopper said, dropping the newspaper and picking up his bat. "I'll do it again." His bandaged hands gripped the bat.

"Sure, sure. How'd you get down here?" Doc Trina held up his eyelid, felt his wrist, and peeled back the edge of the bandage on his cheek. "Heard they had you up at the emergency room. Seems the hospital has a major leak."

Ernesto looked up at the Bopper and his dog dark eyes. They were strong eyes, dark and steady, but today they were not working. Instead of staring, they drifted from woman to woman and then up to the darkening sky.

The Doc took the bat from the Bopper and set it on the ground. "That's better," she said, digging into his shirt pocket. She pulled out a small piece of paper. "A prescription for antibiotics," she said. "Probably came here because Mimi used to take care of this stuff for him." She handed the paper to Antonia. "Maybe you can ask Steamer to help."

"I have money."

"Good, but you'll have to go across town to get the prescription filled. Forget Shorty's by the bank. They'll take forever."

"I will ask Steamer to show me."

As Antonia rested her hand on the Bopper's shoulder, Ernesto rubbed against his ankle. When the Bopper wasn't crazy, he was a good friend willing to share treats. They were good treats, crispy and stinky from rubbish cans all over Hilo, and

Ernesto did not want to lose such a friend, even if he was a dangerous friend who could not be trusted with a bat.

The Doc wiped her hands on her towel-skirt. "You got to stop swinging this bat," she said. "You hear me, Mr. Bopper?"

Ernesto felt the Bopper's bandaged fingers rub the sweet spot behind his ears.

"There is one more thing," Antonia said.

Ernesto watched Antonia and the Doc check Angelica's food bowl and then followed them inside and up the stairs to the orchestra pit. The toolbox was still on the stack of lumber, the hammer and nails right where Mimi had left them. "I need you to hold those boards in place while I nail them to the frame work along the stage."

"That whole stack?" The Doc grabbed the top board. "Must be ten, twenty boards here."

"I cannot do it alone. I would like to surprise Steamer."

"It's been a long day."

"It will only take a moment."

Ernesto leaped to the top of the organ and watched the Doc squat down. She held a board in place while Antonia pounded a nail in each corner. Antonia was a good pounder, using the tap-tap-pound-pound method favored by Mimi. Two soft taps to nudge the nail in place and two good whacks to drive it deep into the wood.

"Easy," Antonia said.

"Reminds me of putting in stitches."

They worked without talking until they reached the center of the stage then they changed places. The Doc tried to skip the tapping and went straight to pounding, a method that bent nails at an alarming rate and caused Antonia to take back the hammer and switch positions.

Sweat dripped down the Doc's face and the small muscles in Antonia's arm bulged but neither woman stopped working. The only sound in the theater was tapping and pounding until Antonia stood up and said, "Finished."

They shook hands, and the Doc said, "This wood has been sitting around for months."

"It will look nice for Steamer's new movie."

They stood together a moment, hands on hips, looking at the Palace.

"There's plenty more work to do," the Doc said.

"Much work."

"Too bad," the Doc said, shaking her head. "Too bad about this place."

Ernesto had not noticed before but the Doc was not good with words. He could see nothing bad about the place.

"I have a small boy," Antonia said.

"Me, I've never had any kids. But I've patched up a few."

"Will he be safe here with Steamer?"

"Unless he crawls into a mailbox. Fellow you got to watch out for is Manny."

"I have heard of him."

"You have?" The Doc gave Antonia a close look. "He's got a boat down at the harbor. Tries to make a living from fishing and running stuff between the islands. Thinks he's living in tramp-steamer days. You watch him if he gets around Papa Joe and Steamer. Three of them together gets crazy."

"There is one more thing."

Ernesto followed the two women to the dressing rooms. A second before the Doc closed the door to keep him out, he saw Antonia lift up her shirt. There were dark bruises on her ribs.

He ran upstairs. He did not know what to do. Whenever he was frightened, eating made him feel safer, so he jumped onto the snack-bar table and gobbled up scraps of tasty ham and mac salad from Doc Trina's plate. When the plate was clean, he blinked. He still did not feel good. Looking for a safe spot to hide from the thought of the woman's bruises, he jumped to the floor, hurried into the ticket booth, and jumped up to Steamer's desk. There he found the paper lined with Antonia's dark blue words.

Dearest Steamer,

This moment is difficult for me. I want you to know these things before anything happens. They'll be here soon. Maybe it's too late already. I do not want anything to hurt you. I would do anything to protect you and Anthony. I want him to be safe. Please. Protect him.

Chapter 20

Steamer rubbed his nose.

The Humane Society office stunk of cat food, dog hair and Ms. Noda. Bundled up in a thick sweater under a leather jacket, she reeked of peanut butter, sardines, and industrial strength disinfectant.

"Patsy," Steamer said. "She's part Siamese, part something else." He made a circle around his eyes with his finger. "Blues eyes and brown mask. Makes her look like a bandit." He pointed behind him. "Lots of thick fur. White tip on her tale."

Mr. Goodmorning rested his elbow on the counter and said, "Everybody knows Patsy."

"I don't know her." Ms. Noda was a heavy woman with a rectangular nametag that identified her as Ms. Jane "Diggie" Noda. Outside, dogs started to bark and kept on barking, an unending mix of small and big barks that Steamer had trained himself not to hear, the same way he had trained himself not to hear roosters and coqui frogs.

"So," Mr. Goodmorning said. "This is where it all starts."

"What?" asked Ms. Noda.

"The dog barking. Can't go anywhere on this island without hearing a dog bark."

Damp air blew through a jagged hole in the room's only clean window.

"Supposed to fix that window," Ms. Noda said, zipping up her jacket. "You from Hilo, right? Kinda figured that from the way you talk. The accents."

"It's a mile down the road," Mr. G said.

"Too cold for t-shirts." Ms. Noda leaned over the counter. "You're wearing t-shirts. Townies, I bet. What you got down there, an animal you dropping off?"

Anthony looked up at her.

"A boy? You can't drop him here."

"We aren't dropping him," Steamer said, pulling Anthony close to him.

"You think we're crazy?" Mr. G buttoned the top button of his white dress shirt while Ms. Noda gave each of them a close look, gave their truck a look too.

"We're trying to find Patsy," Steamer said.

"You the guy from the Palace?"

"We're looking for Patsy," Mr. G said.

"I remember you." Ms Noda popped a Mega Mint into her mouth and washed it down with steaming coffee. "When you going to start showing movies? I went to the Palace the other night. Paper said there was going to be a movie. No movie."

The boy's fingers reached up to grab the top of the counter.

"She disappeared this morning," Steamer said. "We been looking all over town for her."

"I told you that you was going to have trouble with that cat," Ms. Noda said. "Didn't I tell you that? I remember when you came in here with that girl. What was her name?"

None of this bothered Steamer. Over the last few months, he had learned to listen to people the same way he listened to tourists and coqui frogs. In the background.

"Martha? Was that her name? Nice girl. Not from around here."

"From Hilo," Mr. G said. "And this is not a t-shirt."

"That's what I said. A townie. Let me see." Ms. Noda unzipped her jacket. "I'll get it. I'm thinking."

Steamer tried to imagine such a thing happening.

"Pretty girl," Ms. Noda said, "but not too smart about picking cats. I told her that cat was going to be trouble. I've seen cats like that hypnotize small children." She looked down at the boy and winked. "You'd better be careful."

"Don't scare the boy," Mr. G said.

"I can feel stuff like that. Didn't I tell you? You was here with her, Mr. Movieman. Why didn't that girl come with you today?"

Mr. G pushed his way in front of Steamer. "We'll look for ourselves. Just let us in so we can check the cat house."

"No need to get nasty," said Ms. Noda.

Two roosters added their crowing to the dogs barking as Ms. Noda stepped from behind the counter. Steamer watched her scratching the back of her head as she led them out the door and through the compound, past a long line of dog cages. "I can make you a good deal on dogs. Got plenty dogs."

"No, thank you," said Mr. G.

"Everyone should have dogs, at least a couple Dobermans. Supposed to be good guard dogs."

"No thank you," said Anthony.

Steamer held the boy's hand and followed Ms. Noda, who had stopped scratching and was picking at a dirty spot on her jacket sleeve. "Was she wearing a collar?"

Steamer fingered the collar in his pocket.

"That girl didn't like her collar," Mr. G said. "Always taking it off and throwing it away. Independent."

"That's the Siamese in her. As I remember, that cat was part Siamese."

"I believe so," Steamer said, squeezing the boy's hand. He wanted him to see how important it was to be nice to people.

"I knew it," Ms. Noda said. "Didn't I tell you! And part cane cat. Can't trust cane cats."

"I know plenty cane cats," Mr. G said, "and they're all very well behaved, and very bright with good manners."

"Cane cats are wild. I tried to warn her."

Mr. G angled in front of Ms. Noda, waved his hands to get her attention, "Ernesto is a cane cat and he is very well behaved."

Ms. Noda stopped and turned to Steamer, "I got to warn you, Mr. Movie, we're going through a kitty drought."

"Kitty drought?" Mr. G asked.

"It happens." Ms. Noda shrugged, still talking to Steamer. "Certain times of the years cats don't have babies. Others times there's so many we're over stocked. June and May are good months. Forget November and December and January. Those are drought months."

"January," the boy said.

"That's right." Ms. Noda tried to push her hand through her thick, wiry red hair. It didn't work. "But we got plenty adults. You can have all the adults you want."

"Kitty drought," Anthony said.

Mr. G opened his mouth to say something but Steamer cut him off. "We're looking for Patsy. She an adult."

Ms. Noda unlocked the door to the cat house. "People always coming to our Kitty Kastle to look for kittens. You should come back in May if you want kittens. In May we have a 2-for-1 sale."

"May we?" asked Mr. G.

"No need to get smart wit me." Ms. Noda snapped her fingers at Steamer. "I remember now.

You and that girl got two kittens. One with a big head. The grey. How's that grey doing? You lose him too?"

"We didn't lose anybody," Mr. G said. "Patsy ran away."

"He looked like one good fighter with that big head."

"He never fights," said Mr. G.

"Skinny, I bet."

"Sturdy," said Mr. G.

She opened the door but blocked the entrance with her body. "You got two cats already so I'm not going to give you another cat. Unless you want one. If you want one adult cat, you pick one, fill out the forms, pay your $30 to get it fixed, and I'll call you when its time to pick it up."

"Fixed?" Mr. G asked. "They broken?"

Steamer covered the boy's ears.

"Fixed so they can't have babies," Ms. Noda said and stepped inside.

There were two rooms inside the Kitty Kastle. One on the right for adults. One on the left for kittens. The drought had produced too many kittens for Steamer to count. Tigers, calicos, blacks, orange and whites, spotted and solids, long hairs and short hairs, a little gray, and three brown-and-white bruisers, all fighting to get at a single bowl of food.

Anthony pointed his finger while he counted, "Twenty-one, twenty-two, twenty-three..."

When Steamer stuck his finger through the chain-link fence, the skinny gray left the line to the food bowl to investigate. Steamer poked at the gray's protruding ribs. Four times he nudged the gray away from the chain link, four times it came back to him.

"Like I said, we going through a drought, but there are always plenty of adults." Ms. Noda shook the chain-link fence on the right. "Plenty nice adult cats."

Each adult had a separate cage. None of them looked happy. They stayed in the back of their cages, staring out of their captivity, as far from the humans as they could get. Steamer tried not to look at them.

"Gentle, these cats," Ms. Noda said. "Most of them had owners but something happened. Who knows what? People come and go. Like you."

"No Patsy here," Mr. G said, bending over to search the bottom row of cages.

"No Patsy," said the boy.

Ms. Noda tried to push her hand through her hair again. "You should take one."

"We got two," said Mr. G.

"Can't leave them in these cages forever. We don't like to say what we do with them. But I can tell you."

Steamer covered the boy's ears as Ms. Noda explained the policy about adult cats and how long they could be kept. There were just too many. No one wanted adult cats, just kittens. If they stayed too long, well, they were put away.

"Put away where?" the boy asked.

Ms. Noda patted him on the head and said, "You never mind about that."

Steamer reached into his pocket and held Patsy's collar as tight as he could, afraid for her and everyone else. Then he saw Mimi lift the latch to the kitty cage and slip inside, using her rubber slipper to push back the little grey as it tried to escape. Gently, she scooped up a brown-and-white with blue eyes and held it out to Steamer. Part Siamese, she said.

Poking his finger through the cage, he rubbed the kitten's fluffy white belly. The soft fur felt like clouds. She'll make a good Hilo cat, Mimi said. If she can stay out of trouble.

Steamer remembered Mimi telling him Patsy's life story, how she was from Volcano and all her thick fur came from a long line of Volcano cats, from an old family of artists and scientists, who studied the volcano and loved the cold air high on the mountain.

Steamer smelled cat food and litter boxes while Mimi pointed at the white spot at the tip of Patsy's tail and said, "She has a very sophisticated tail."

"An exclamation point," Steamer said. "Like at the end of a story."

"Hey," Mr. G said, and Steamer felt him grab his shoulder, shake him. Then he heard Ms. Noda say, "If you don't want no real cats, just kittens we don't have, I guess it's time for you to go back to Honolulu."

They followed her out the door and nobody said anything until they were back sitting in Mr. G's truck. The boy knelt between them, looking out the back window at the animals in their cages.

"Big cats didn't look too happy," Mr. G said, and pulled the starter. "They're waiting for their owners."

"Their owners put them there," said the boy.

Steamer and Mr. G looked at the boy and then back at the Kitty Kastle. Letting the engine idle, Mr. G covered the boy's ears. "They're going to fix all those kittens so they can't have babies?"

Steamer nodded. "That's the rule."

"Not even one litter?"

"No."

"And Ernesto, he no can?"

"Fixed."

"And Patsy?"

"Fixed."

Mr. Goodmorning took his hands off the boy's ears and gripped the steering wheel. "Cats got it tough."

"Better fixed than being dead," the boy said.

Steamer braced his feet against the rusting metal. It was going to be a rough ride home.

"Heck, you don't need kittens to be a cat," Mr. G said. "I don't have any kids." He stepped on the gas, missed a parked car, nicked the Humane Society's mailbox, and stopped at the road, held in check by a long line of bumper-to-bumper traffic. "And I'm okay."

Ms. Noda was standing in the parking lot, watching them.

"She's not so bad," Mr. G said, sticking his hand out the window and waving to her. "Thought she was crazy at first."

"Still think she's crazy," Steamer said.

"Just trying to move the merchandise. Help those adults." A gap appeared in the line of cars, Mr. G jammed the stick shift, and the truck lurched into traffic. "Adults need help too."

The boy looked out the back window and watched the Kat Kastle grow smaller and smaller. "We can come back tonight," the boy said.

Steamer watched the boy's tiny hands press against the glass.

"We can save them," Mr. G said. "We can cut through the fence and set them free."

"I am small so I can go through small spaces," the boy said. "I can get inside."

"I'll handle the speedy getaway, like Steve McQueen."

"Can't take care of all those cats," Steamer said. "Can't break other people's property."

For a long moment they rode in silence, then the boy said, "That is true."

When the Humane Society was out of sight, Mr. G downshifted and swung into the slow lane. "This boy is like Mimi," he said. "Wild for a little guy."

The boy gave up on the window and sat between them with his hands on his knees. The three of them settled into not talking, listening to the wind rush through the windows. Steamer thought about Mimi as the truck passed the airport and turned left on the road that would take them to the Palace. When they drove past Suisan and Club Next to Last Call, they saw the lights go out and heard a window break.

"Antman," Mr. Goodmorning said.

"What?" asked Steamer.

"That's what we should call him."

"Who?"

"The boy," Mr. Goodmorning said. "He's like one superhero who can crawl through small spaces. That's his special power. And he can leave trails of cookies and lift ten times his body weight. And tell when things are true or not."

"Patsy," the boy said, pointing into the dark.

"And see things that no one else can see," Mr. Goodmorning said, stepping on the gas to help the old truck plow through a cloud of "Witchy Woman."

Chapter 21

Patsy grasped the kitten tightly in her mouth as she zigzagged through the double line of people stretching from Bay Front to the Palace. Searching for the path of least resistance, she navigated between and around leather sandals, tennis shoes and rubber slippers.

"7:45!" said a man wearing orange clogs.

"Line's not moving," said green slippers.

"Can't trust Movieman," said heavy boots. "Always losing cats"

Breathing hard, Patsy slipped by jeans and nylons. Through the smell of mold and cigarettes, incense and stale beer, she searched for a familiar voice.

It was not easy to carry a kitten, even one this small, and Patsy could not imagine how Angelica managed six of the small creatures. She stopped in front of Mr. Goodmorning's doorway and sat between four black shoes that supported two men as big as pier pilings.

"Nothing yet."

"He'll show."

"Let's wait across the street."

In the neon glow, heads craned left and right. Hands dug deep into pockets as the boa-constrictor line bulged and grew. Shifting her grip on the kitten's tiny neck, Patsy smelled popcorn and butter. She turn left and squeezed through the elongated beast.

"What the heck is *Fatal Desire*?" said a pair of extra-large rubber slippers.

"It's a love story with a whale and Humphrey Bogart."

Patsy turned into the alley, checked behind the dumpster but found no Angelica, just two bowls with food and water. She could not leave the kitten without a mother.

In the darkness at the back of the Palace, two black shoes protruded from a cloud of deodorant smell that reminded Patsy of gas stations and shopping malls. As she stepped closer to her secret door, she told herself that she preferred the patchouli smell of Mr. Goodmorning and the people who came to the Palace in tie-dyed shirts. She looked up at a stomach hanging over a belt, stopped to consider its massive girth, and darted into the Palace, careful not to brush against this chemical-drenched stranger.

Happy to be home, she moved easily up the dark stairwell, smelling Ernie and Steamer and a woman. A soapy woman. She ran through the curtains into the dim light of the main theater. Snoring loudly, Doc Trina was slumped over the pipe organ. Was she wearing a pink t-shirt? Before Patsy had time to investigate, a strange woman came out of the projection booth and hurried down the aisle.

Patsy ducked under a seat, repositioned the kitten, and sniffed for Ernie. He was somewhere close, hidden behind the smell of burning butter and jasmine soap. As the woman's black high-tops passed in the aisle, Patsy thought she heard the patter of Ernesto's paws on the concrete floor. The woman stopped and looked back at the theater. She was inches from Patsy, and Patsy could hear her breathing, feel the warmth inside her.

"I won't forget you," the woman whispered. "I love you."

Patsy closed her eyes, held the kitten as tight as she could, and waited for the magic words to change everything. She heard the Doc's snoring and felt the kitten's tiny heartbeat. When she opened her eyes, she saw only shadows. The woman had disappeared. Patsy made a note to herself that once she had found a safe place for her kitten, she would hurry back to help Ernie keep an eye on this woman who moved like Mimi and used the magic words to avoid detection.

She ran up the aisle, by the projection booth, and down the stairs to the lobby. Mr. Goodmorning was standing in the snack bar, grilling red dogs and fluffing a cloud of popcorn. Melting butter sizzled in an old tin frying pan.

"Patsy!" Mr. Goodmorning shouted, and ran from behind the counter. He picked her up and hugged her, pressing her tightly to his chest. She liked his patchouli smell. "What you got here?" He kissed her between the ears. "Oh, good work. You solved the kidnapping. I'm busy or I'd say hello. Lots of work to do." He carried her into the ticket booth and set her down on the counter. "Look who's here."

Steamer hopped out of his chair, in the process tipping over a pile of quarters. While a small boy watched, he hugged and kissed her. "Good girl," Steamer said. "Good girl. Where'd you get the kitty?"

"One drought," the boy said.

"Solved the mystery of the kidnapping," said Mr. Goodmorning. Then he whispered, "Remember, what I told you. Don't say anything about subtitles"

"But there are subtitles."

"That doesn't mean you have to broadcast the news."

"The truth is good," said the boy.

"And don't worry about the trustees," Mr. Goodmorning said, heading back to the snack bar. "I got my buddy Babette picking them up at the airport. They'll be here right on time."

Through the mouse hole in the ticket window, a mouth covered with thick red lipstick said, "Please, Steamer, can we start the movie? I can't remember ever having to wait this long."

"Just a moment, please," the boy said.

Patsy sniffed the boy. He smelled of red dogs and Oreos and the woman Patsy had seen inside the Palace. A soapy smell.

"Now that Patsy's here," Steamer said, "we can start the movie."

"Ten pounds," the boy said

Patsy liked this boy but she did not let go of her kitten. Something about the night and the long bulging line scared her. Everything was not perfect. Something was missing.

The boy pointed at the cash box and said, "She needs a home."

"Perfect." Steamer emptied the bills onto the counter and padded the cashbox with missing-cat fliers. Gently, he took the kitty from Patsy's mouth and placed it in the box.

The three of them watched the kitten sleeping.

"Good kitten," said Steamer.

"One pound," said the boy.

Patsy yawned. She was sleepy and happy and thought she could feel the little kitten inside her.

Steamer took the list out of his pocket and crossed out the line about finding Patsy. "One more down," he said. "We're ready."

"Ready," the boy said to Patsy.

"Ready to continue the long tradition of selling our creations for money so we can eat. Right, Patsy?"

A drop of sweat rolled down Steamer's cheek, and Patsy noticed he was wearing his work clothes. A faded pair of jeans and a Sig-Zane shirt with a collar. Both pressed. The boy was wearing a white dress shirt and pressed jeans with high-top sneakers.

"Oh," Steamer said. "This is Antman. He has super powers."

The boy rubbed Patsy's back, touched the sleeping kitty. "Thick fur," he said. "Hilo cat." He patted Patsy's shoulder. "Good girl."

Patsy thought he was quick and sharp-eyed like a cat. She looked from him to the still-growing line outside the window. A grey-haired woman pressed her hand against the glass and said, "Steamer, can we buy snacks before the we buy tickets?"

Patsy felt the boy pick her up and place her in his lap. He patted her head softly. He had tiny hands that fit neatly between her ears. She had worked hard and now she was tired. She would rest here, just a moment.

"I'm starving," the woman said. "What time does the movie start?"

"7:30" said Steamer.

"It's 7:50."

"The Palace regrets any inconvenience our customers might experience." Steamer pointed at the clock behind him. Its arms had stopped at 7:29. "One senior," he said. "$6.50."

"Why do you think I'm a senior?"

"One adult. $7.50."

"Give me the senior."

"We got red dogs tonight," Steamer said.

"And plenty butter," the boy said, ripping a ticket from a huge roll and handing it through the window.

"Last time I ate butter and popcorn, I was a little kid," the woman said.

"Butter is good," said the boy.

Patsy watched Mr. Goodmorning pull the chrome handle of the ancient popcorn popper. A river of popcorn spilled out of the steel bucket and piled up against glass doors held shut by duct tape. The counter display was packed with M&M's, Tootsie Rolls, Spicy Squid, and arare crunchers.

Ticket in hand, the woman shuffled off to the snack bar, and the next customer said, "It's good to see you back, Steamer."

Patsy gave her a close look. She was the thin woman with mildly blond hair who came everyday to the gym next door where she pedaled bicycles that went nowhere. "The last time I was here, you didn't look too happy" the woman said, "But you showed a wonderful love story."

"*To Have and Have Not,*" Steamer said.

"That's it. I like the ending. Except for the smoking."

"Old days," said the boy.

Steamer smiled and handed her a ticket. The boy collected her money. And Patsy made a note that this boy called Antman was a good worker. Like Mimi, he did not let Steamer forget the important steps of a process.

A man with no fur on his head but a curly patch of it on his chin stepped to the window. Steamer covered Patsy's ears a second before the man boomed, "One senior!"

He slid his money through the mouse hole and in return the boy gave him a blue ticket. The man was walking away when he snapped his fingers and turned to shout, "Did you hear that Papa Joe has a picture bride? A young one."

"Not true, Professor," said Steamer.

"Not true," shouted Mr. Goodmorning.

"Came into town this morning," the Professor shouted. "Remember that movie you showed about picture brides?"

"*Picture Bride*," Steamer said.

"That's it. Beautiful. Nothing wrong with wanting a woman," the Professor shouted. "A man has needs."

"Please," Steamer pointed at Anthony. "Not around the boy."

Patsy blinked. She did not trust the Professor. In the flat world when a man said he had needs that meant he was about to create a huge monster or fire a missile that would turn into a mushroom cloud.

"Get over here," Mr. Goodmorning shouted. "Plenty of good snacks take care of your needs."

Patsy felt herself getting sleepy. Even though Steamer kept feeding tiny pieces of blue paper through the mouse hole, the line kept getting bigger. If he wanted it to go away so he could go to sleep in the comfortable darkness of the Palace, he should stop feeding it. Patsy closed her eyes.

"What's playing?" a voice with tuna breath asked. "I mean, I know what the poster says but I want to know what's playing."

Patsy knew this voice. One of Ernie's friends, he liked movies with explosions and always brought small bags of tasty snacks, usually spicy hot cuttlefish, sometimes sweet rice candy. As soon as he was settled in his seat, he would tear them open, chomp as quickly as he could, and then, if the movie did not have an explosion in the first five minutes, he would fall quickly to sleep. He was a good sleeper and Ernie liked to balance on his huge stomach while sampling from his snack packs.

"CasaNoir Fatal Desire," Steamer said.

"Any action?"

"Three hours of beautiful cinematography punctuated by five minutes of whale arrival."

"Does anybody get killed?"

"No, but some Nazis make a few threats. And I threw in some karate stuff. The part where the lead guy explains why he's given up fighting."

"Those old karate movies were good. I liked the dubbing. Voices coming out after the lips stop moving."

"No dubbing here. Only subtitles."

"Jeez, you really know how to spoil a party. Any explosions?"

"No. But a whale appears out of nowhere."

"Can you wake me when that whale's about to happen? I'll be sleeping in the third row"

"Sleep is good," the boy said.

"I like to sleep," the old man said.

"$7.50," said the boy.

This boy is remarkable thought Patsy.

The snack-eating explosion man said, "I heard you got yourself a new girlfriend?"

"Not me."

"Who's the boy?"

"Antman," the boy said. "My mother is not a girlfriend."

Patsy smelled milk and opened her eyes to see a woman with a small child balanced on her hip nudge the man out of the way and shove three crumpled bills through the mouse hole. Steamer pushed them back at her. "Keep it. Movie's on me. I hope your kids like it. I cut out all the violence."

"They like violence."

"I threw in some old karate stuff. It's subtitled. No dubbing. Very authentic."

Patsy looked at the woman and her child. She did not know why but she wanted to say the magic words. She looked at the kitten in the cashbox and the boy called Antman. She felt the magic words growing inside her.

Love, Patsy tried to say.

As the woman walked inside with two children following her, Mr. Goodmorning stuck his head through the box office door. "Every seat in the house is full" He nodded at the line that still reached back to Bay front. "Don't know what we're going to do now."

The next customer, a bulky woman with a red hat, asked, "Did you say the movie was subtitled?"

"Only a small part," Steamer said.

"Subtitles," she hissed, sending the dreaded word down the line, from the box office to the ocean.

Subtitles. Subtitles. Subtitles.

"Did someone say subtitles?"

Subtitles. Subtitles. Subtitles.

"Crap!" shouted the last person, his back to the ocean, as the line broke into a hundred pieces, spilled onto the road, and swirled around a Hilo Taxi that was struggling to reach the curb.

Love, Patsy tried to say. Love

Magically, at that exact moment, the taxi's doors swung open, the Palace's five trustees stepped out, and the crowd swept them away into the night.

lz

Chapter 22

Papa Joe was sitting on the

Manila Queen, listening to Manny read Johnny's letter out loud to Teresa. She was looking up at the stars, and Papa Joe was remembering the bar fight and how Teresa had shoved her way through the crowd.

Without her, they wouldn't have escaped. She had pulled Manny and him to the bathroom. She had stood on the toilet seat and used her elbow to knock out what was left of the window. Then she had helped them climb through, before climbing through herself and using Manny's penlight to guide them along a narrow path between rusting machinery to the front door of the Iron Works.

Only when they had reached the safety of the bridge did she stop to say, "Lucky my second man was one welder. Know all the ways in and out of that place."

Sirens swirled in flashes of bright light as the police cars arrived and the cops arrested everyone who came out of the Second to Last Call, including the bartender. Manny's two cop friends were the last to leave, sitting in the back of an ambulance and shaking their heads.

Yes, Teresa was a good woman. She had saved them. He handed her a box of Girl Scout Cookies, the peanut butter kine, her favorites.

She was eating her third cookie when Manny put down the letter and picked up Big Black. He stroked the cat's head and thought a long time before he said, "Lot's of stuff in that letter."

They sat in the candlelight and nodded.

"Johnny asked me to take care of her so I got to take care of her."

"Lots of avenues here," Manny said. "We need to ask the Madonna for advice."

"How you going to do that?" Teresa asked, examining all sides of a peanut butter cookie before angling its four corners into her mouth.

While Manny scratched his head, Papa Joe thought of the Madonna at the Pink Church and his Madonna at the Empire.

"We should work awhile," Teresa said. "Working makes me think good."

"That's a good idea," Manny said. "While we're working, the Madonna might show up. She's the patron saint of workers."

So Papa Joe helped Teresa and Manny unload ninety-seven boxes of Girl Scout cookies from Manny's boat and stack them on the dock while he thought about Antonia and her boy Anthony and what he would ask the Madonna.

"Only short a box or two," Manny said.

"Or three," said Teresa. "Maybe the Madonna can make up the difference."

"Plenty room now," Manny said. "Ready for sea."

They stood on the dock, looking at the boat riding high in the water and listening to the wind in the Banyan tree, until Manny said, "Good night for sailing."

Teresa picked up Big Black and held him in her arms, dug her thick fingers through his fur. "You ask me, a woman taking care of her kid can't be all bad. Any Madonna worth her weight will tell you the same thing."

"The Golden Madonna got plenty weight," Manny said.

Papa Joe looked up at the star-filled sky and said, "I figure I'll go back to the Empire and see if I can squeeze anything out my Madonna."

As sirens tore at the night, Big Black jumped from Teresa's arms and Manny picked up the biggest crate of cookies. He carried it back aboard the *Manila Queen*. "Just in case," he said. "Can't go sailing without supplies. You go see what your Madonna has to say and I'll anchor out in the bay to wait for further instructions."

Papa Joe walked with Teresa back over the bridge and along the beach until they reached town and saw a light on at Lizard Mama. It was Sunday night, and Papa Joe had never before seen a light on at the Lizard Mama on a Sunday night. He took this as a sign and asked Teresa to go inside with him even though she was a firm believer that the Lizard Mama was too expensive for most people. When she finally agreed, just this once because she too had never seen the Lizard Mama open on Sunday, Papa Joe took that as another sign.

Ten minutes later, he stepped from the well-lit interior of the Lizard Mama to the darkness outside, carrying an extra-wide double futon on his shoulder. He was thinking about sleep and how he didn't care what the Madonna said because the woman and boy needed a good night of sleeping and a place to stay that wasn't floating in the middle of the ocean with his friend Manny Matos at the helm. He wanted her to stay at the Palace for a good night of sleeping, and in the morning he would take the boy surfing.

"What you thinking about?" Teresa asked, walking out behind him, a single futon on her shoulder.

"Sleeping."

"I sleep three hours a night, tops. How much you sleep?"

"Some nights I don't sleep."

"A man like you should sleep good."

"Some nights I go to sleep and don't wake up for two days. I got an old army cot."

"I seen it."

"It's up by the air vents in the balcony. A good place for sleeping. I like an open place for sleeping"

"I know plenty men like to sleep on cots. My first boy's father, the welder at the Iron Works, he liked a cot."

"A cot is good for one person."

"Not good for two people."

"Not good."

"Me and my welder broke our backs trying to sleep that way."

Even with the futon on his back, Papa Joe was walking his regular pace, but Teresa passed him. He watched her move ahead while she rolled her futon from one shoulder to the other. "You one strong girl," he said.

"I got one strong head."

"You got a strong back. And a good punch."

Teresa waited for him to catch up, and then said, "You know me."

"What you weigh? A hundred forty, maybe a hundred fifty?"

"Maybe one seventy."

"A woman your size makes me feel young again."

"You not so old."

He knew that was a lie, but he did not mind her saying it. He walked with her, shoulder-to-shoulder, thinking of her thick arms, heavy breasts, and strong legs. The breeze ruffled the palms. When they turned the corner and headed up the street toward the Palace, a big man stepped out of the shadows and said, "How you doing, Joe."

The street was empty, quiet, and they were standing a few buildings away from the Palace's neon glow. Papa Joe said, "You know me?"

"Sure. I know you. Your name is Joe, and we're looking for this woman." The man showed him a black-and-white photo of Antonia. "You seen her around?"

Papa Joe figured he weighed a couple hundred pounds. Another big man stepped out from the shadows and blocked Teresa.

"We're looking for her," the man with the photo said, holding it closer to Papa Joe's face.

"Can't see nothing in the dark."

"What you got there?" the second man asked Teresa.

"Nothing for you."

The man with the photo pointed it at Teresa, and asked, "You seen her?"

"That one pretty girl. Too young for you."

"You seen her?"

"I seen her now."

Papa Joe liked being here with Teresa. She was a good woman and they were sitting on the bow of a boat cutting through a storm.

The man stuffed the picture in his pocket. "Maybe we should go up to your place. Better light in there. You can see the photo."

"That's where we're going even without you," Teresa said.

They stayed on the Empire side of the street, Papa Joe being careful not to step on cracks.

"What you doing with all those futons?"

"Two people, two futons," Teresa said.

"This your new bride?" the other man said. "People in line for the movie said Papa Joe had a picture bride."

"That's me," Teresa said.

"You kinda old to be in a picture."

They stopped at the door to the Empire, and Papa Joe unlocked the door, reached inside to turn on the lights. "You're a couple of big fellows," he said. "I figure each of you weighs about 150, 160."

"Get in!"

They dumped the futons on the floor, and Papa Joe saw a new bottle of tequila and the shoebox on his desk. One of the big men said something about his friend in Honolulu losing a lot of money while Papa Joe read his own name on a piece of lined notebook paper folded under the shoebox. When he looked up, the two big guys were standing in front of the desk looking down. Teresa was leaning against the wall, near the umbrella stand.

"Maybe you should go talk to your friend," Teresa said. "Maybe he knows where the girl in your picture is."

"He's not talking anymore."

Papa Joe sat at the desk, and asked, "How about a drink?" He poured double shots into four coffee cups. "To your friend."

The picture of Antonia landed on the desk.

"You seen her?"

"I figure she weighs maybe 100," said Papa Joe.

"Girls at the club said she had a boyfriend who bragged about his uncle in Hilo. We figure that's you, Joe."

The four of them drank, then Papa Joe poured another round of shots. The men were still standing close to the desk. Theresa had edged closer to the umbrella stand.

"There's a reward, Joe."

Papa Joe finished his tequila.

"You seen her, Joe?" The man pushed the picture toward Papa Joe. "Lot of money missing, Joe. We get the girl and the money, we go away. You and your new wife can go across the street and see a movie. Hear they got a good one over there. A love story."

"Don't like love stories," Teresa said.

"I like a good love story," the man said. "As long as it has some sex scenes. And some action."

"I like action," Teresa said.

The man doing most of the talking picked up the shoebox, shook it, and looked at the note on the desk. "You got a letter there, Joe."

Papa Joe took his time pouring another shot into his coffee cup.

"Go ahead. Read it to us."

Papa Joe took his time folding open the paper, spreading it on the desk, and taking a sip of his tequila before he started to read.

> *Dear Papa Joe,*
> *I hope you understand. I never wanted to hurt Johnny, and I do not want to hurt you. It is true, I do not love Johnny. I would have told him the truth but there was no time and he is not a man who understands easily. I hope you will understand for him.*

Men paid me and I did whatever they asked. Johnny knew that. He would come in the evenings and I would sit with him and watch the other girls dance. We would listen to music and talk. I held his hand and made him feel he was not alone. That is what he needed. He was alone in the world and men do not like to feel alone. He paid me and I did what he asked. He knew that, but men see only what they want to see. You understand, Papa Joe, don't you?

I tell you these things because I want you to know the truth. Johnny is a gentle man and I treated him with respect. I never hurt him and I want him always to be safe. But I do not love him. I cannot say what could have been. I'll only know what happened and what is happening now.

I say these things because I must ask you to help me one more time. There is only one person I love. My boy. Anthony.

Papa Joe stopped reading and folded the letter. He poured another drink and left it on the desk. Teresa was looking at him and the big guy was holding the shoebox open.

"Lotta money here, Joe, but this isn't all of it."

"Nice girl you protecting. You didn't finish the letter, Joe. Why don't you finish the letter? We want to hear it."

Teresa's grabbed the UH umbrella.

"Maybe we should take a look around. Maybe go over to the movie place, see who is over there."

"You aren't going anywhere," Papa Joe said.

Chapter 23

E rnesto shook his head to chase away the memories. There were so many of them he was certain Patsy had returned to the Palace, but he did not have time to search for her. He was busy clinging to the edge of the roof, watching Antonia step up to the ladder.

She was quick and agile, and he respected her balance, but he did not want to let her go. Through the rungs of Mimi's ladder he could see the alley below and the top of Dumpster Kicker's head. Before the movie had started, Ernesto had seen this man kick the dumpster three times and laugh at Angelica when she scurried off with two kittens in her mouth.

Ernesto had rushed inside to tell the woman about this new danger and found her crying in the projection booth, her tears a sure sign that she already knew about the brutal scene in the alley. He had watched her hang Mimi's rosary beads on the projector, tape the Bopper's prescription to the wall, and sit for endless moments at Steamer's desk.

When she had run down the aisle, he had followed her, staying under the empty seats and fighting off patches of memories growing stronger. Until she had stopped suddenly, looked down and said to him, "I won't forget you. I love you."

Now, on the roof, he shook his head. He needed it clear. No more memories. At this second, he was leaning over the ledge while Antonia stepped onto the ladder. Through the rungs, he saw the other player in the chase game. The Dumpster-Kicker was down in the alley, guarding the back door and watching both ends of the alley.

Ernesto believed he had finally won the chase game. The woman had nowhere to go. The ladder was too dangerous. She would have to turn around and go back inside. If they hurried, they could sit in the darkness with the flat people and eat leftover snacks.

A yellow moon appeared and shed bright light on the woman's face. She had eyes like Mimi's and in them he saw great courage. She did not hesitate. Instead of going on all fours like a cat, she stepped onto the ladder human fashion, and walked across, stepping from rung to rung without looking down, stopping only once, at the middle, to steady herself when the ladder sagged.

Ernesto looked down, saw the big chaser, then something else, something in the shadows, moving slow but hidden too deep even for a cat's eyes to see. When Ernesto gave up trying to see what could not be seen, he looked up. The woman was across to the other side. She stepped onto the fire escape, climbed down, up and over a railing, and pressed herself against the building. Slowly she moved along the ledge toward Mr. Goodmorning's window.

Ernesto thought of Patsy and Mimi and how many times they had gone this way. They had crossed a hundred times. He had crossed the ladder once. It was not true what the flat people said about the first time being the hardest. He had crossed once and now he could not make his legs move. She was getting away. He watched the woman open the window, crawl inside, and look back at the Palace. Ernesto had lost one woman, he was not about to lose another. He dug his claws into the wood, ran to the middle of the ladder, looked down, and his paw slipped. The woman held out her arms, and he jumped.

For a moment Ernesto felt the night split open and the moon freeze inside him. He was falling. Then the woman caught him and pressed him to her chest. He felt her fingers on his ribs, felt her heart beating. Was this how the chase game ended?

"Where do you think you're going?" she whispered. "You must stay here to take care of Anthony. My brave man, little Ernesto." She set him down on the windowsill. "That's an order."

Ernesto felt scared, good, happy and insane.

"You go home, Ernesto."

She moved out of the Palace's green glow, feeling her way as if she were blind, her arms in front of her searching the darkness for the other side of the room. Ernesto ran to the door and waited while she stepped warily across the floor. He meowed twice and twice more until she changed direction, reached out and grabbed the doorknob.

Her eyes were not as good as his in the dark, but she was better with doors and knew their secrets of opening and closing. She was through in an instant, and Ernesto followed her black high tops down the stairs, jumped ahead of her, then stopped at the next door. When she opened it just a crack, a sliver of neon light cut across the dark hallway.

Ernesto saw a black car stop in front of the Empire. Two men got out and stood on the sidewalk. Ernesto had seen men like this in the flat world. They were too slow to be chasers but they were good at blocking escape routes. They could stand for endless hours with their arms crossed, saying stupid things until they grabbed a runner by the neck.

Without breathing, Ernesto peeked further out the door. The lights were on at the Empire. Someone was sitting at Papa Joe's desk. The night was so still he could hear the audience in the Palace breathing. If the woman was smart and wanted to win this chase game, she should go left into the darkness, follow the sidewalk to the ocean. No one would catch her there. But he did not want her to escape. He wanted her to go back to the Palace.

The two big blockers waved to someone at the Palace, then the bigger one stood in front of the door to the Empire while the other one disappeared around the corner into Papa Joe's vacant lot. Ernesto recognized these movements from chase games in the flat world, where they were called standard procedure.

"What the hell!" a deep voice shouted from Angelica's alley.

The big blocker ran across the street toward the Palace. As soon as he passed into the alley's darkness, Antonia whispered, "You go home, Ernesto." She rubbed his head, then stepped into the street and ran toward the Empire.

Ernesto wanted to tell her that she was going in the wrong direction. Escape was the other way, toward the ocean, but she was strong and quick like Patsy, and by the time he thought these things she was already across the street, out of reach and moving fast.

Ernesto stepped onto the sidewalk. She reached the Empire and banged on the front door. "Open up!" she shouted. "Police!" The lights went out, glass broke, and Antonia banged on the door once more before disappearing into the vacant lot.

Ernesto heard something crash into the dumpster behind him, but he did not look back. He shot across the street, heard Teresa shout "Pervert!" and stopped at the corner of the Empire. The vacant lot was overgrown with maile pilau. Its stinky leaves covered a rusting tractor, piles of moldy bricks, and a slab of concrete left over from the tsunami.

Where was Antonia?

The clouds broke, and the moon shed a flimsy light on a scene that reminded Ernesto of wars in the flat world when sparkling flares caught shadowy figures caught in barbwire. A big blocker was standing at the side door of the Empire. Antonia had stopped in the middle of the lot, behind the overturned tractor. Smart like a cat, she was following the stay-still rule. When trapped in the open, blinded by light, remain perfectly still! Blend into your surroundings! Wait for darkness to return!

In this moment of stillness, the doors to the Palace swung open and the Antman ran out. Instead of following the best chase-game tactics, he stopped only for a moment, long enough for his catlike eyes to find his mother in the moonlight. He waved to her and waved again as he ran straight for her. Not ducking low or dodging left, just running straight and high.

Hide! Get in the shadows! Ernie wanted to shout but the words did not come to him. He could only meow and squeak, and that was not enough to make the boy change course. While the big blocker tore through maile pilau and crashed through rusted junk, the Antman jumped into his mother's arms.

Ernesto felt the earth move, a tremble. The moon disappeared behind the clouds, and for a moment he was alone in the dark. He heard heavy breathing. Then his keen eyes adjusted and the darkness gave way to the faint glow of the Palace's neon sign. The earth shook.

The woman was hugging the boy to her chest. A few feet from her, the big blocker was climbing over the tractor, reaching out to grab her neck. The Antman waved his mighty fist.

Ernesto charged. He climbed over two rusted shopping carts, jumped to the top of a sagging refrigerator, and leaped into the air, hook claws pointed at the big man's face. The blocker's arm went up and swung right, caught Ernesto on the side of the head and shot him through the air like a baseball. Ernesto felt the world spinning, momentum building. The Empire was growing bigger, bigger. He swung his legs, closed his eyes, and slammed into the wall of the Empire, slid to the ground.

Lying on his side, he wondered if this was the way the chase game was supposed to end. He felt the earth open up and saw the Bopper rise up, run toward the tractor. With a bandage on his head, a bat on his shoulder, the Bopper shouted, "I did it. I'll do it again."

The big blocker reached behind his back. The Bopper cocked his bat and charged. Ernesto saw Antonia and her boy running toward the Empire, heard a shot and a *thwack*. Looked back and saw the blocker on the ground, the Bopper standing over him with his bat in the air.

"I did it. I'll do it again."

Ernesto crawled toward the Empire. He closed his eyes. He did not want to see what was going to happen. He felt the woman scoop him up and put him in the boy's arms. He felt the boy's heart beating. He felt the earth tremble. He felt his heart growing bigger.

Chapter 24

Steamer opened his eyes.

As the credits rolled, he saw that he was alone in the theater except for Doc Trina. She was still slumped over the pipe organ, still snoring.

He felt Patsy rub against his leg.

How long had he been sleeping? The audience had whistled and clapped when the Whale Rider broke through the Casablanca fog and carried away two Nazis. They had cheered when a double-hull canoe packed with Maoris ran over a harpoon-wielding Gregory Peck. Cheered again when the *African Queen* delivered a karate-kicking Bruce Lee to save Bogie from Ingrid Bergman. Sighed when he escaped into the fog with Lauren Bacall wearing a checkered suit and saying in a deep voice, "You know how to whistle, don't you? Just put your lips together and blow."

Steamer smiled. He loved that ending. He was certain that Bogie would rather whistle with Lauren than walk with Claude Rains and mutter, "Louis, I think this is the beginning of a beautiful friendship."

Claude Rains or Lauren Bacall? Friendship or love?

He felt Patsy rub against his ankle, and he remembered holding Mimi in his arms. Where was she now? "Don't worry," he said, reaching down to rub Patsy. "We'll find her."

The floor shook, and Patsy skittered away, down the stairs toward the lobby.

"What the heck!" Doc Trina shouted, sitting up at the pipe organ.

As Steamer stumbled out of the projection booth, he heard sirens screaming and dogs barking and horns honking. A circle of stragglers that included Ms. Noda, the Professor, and the five trustees were standing by the snack bar eating red dogs and popcorn. When Mr. Goodmorning brought over a tray of cokes and said something about happy endings, they broke into loud laughter.

Steamer stopped behind Ms. Noda.

"Great movie," she said, squeezing a thick line of ketchup onto a shriveled red dog.

Watching her closely, the Professor said, "You remind me of someone." As she raised the red dog to her mouth, he followed up by asking, "Are you from around here?"

Ms. Noda bit into the red dog, chewed and swallowed, then pointed what was left of the bun at the street. "Lots of action out there."

The main body of the audience had spilled into the street, most of them laughing, slapping each other on the back, only to be stopped by a line of policemen. As a thick and heavy vog drifted through the street turning the moon yellow, making it hard to breathe, Steamer struggled to get through the crowd.

Doc grabbed his shoulder. "Jeez," she said. "I go to sleep for a minute and look what happens."

Steamer looked for the boy, saw two police cars and an ambulance parked in front of the Empire. A cop in yellow rain gear was holding a shoebox and talking to Papa Joe. Two medics wheeled a gurney past them. While the big body strapped under a white sheet rolled its head back and forth, the medics lifted the gurney and shoved it into the ambulance. Teresa backed out of the Empire, dragging somebody by the elbows. Each of the medics grabbed an ankle and helped Teresa heave her load into the ambulance.

A second ambulance whooped out of the alley next to the Palace, its red lights and siren opening a hole through the crowd. It turned right, stopped in front of the Palace, and its door swung open. The driver called to Doc Trina. Still wearing her pink "Club Fem Nu" t-shirt, she leaned inside and listened to the driver say that they had picked up two guys in the alley and now they were going across the street to get one more from the vacant lot. Could she come along to help?

The Doc turned to Steamer and held out her hand. "Interesting movie." she said. "I didn't think you had it in you."

"You slept through it."

"But I heard it."

They shook hands, and Steamer thought she had strong hands, like Mimi's. He looked down to see Patsy sitting at his feet. Together they watched the Doc squeeze into the front seat of the ambulance. With the door hanging open and its red lights flashing, it moved slowly through the crowd, hopped the curb, and drove into the empty lot.

"You the movie guy?"

Steamer turned to see a young cop holding a flashlight and clipboard. Behind him, Antonia was holding a statue over her head and pushing her way through the crowd, headed toward the ocean. The cop flashed the light in Steamer's face. "You're the movie guy, right?"

"That's me."

"Mimi and me used to be classmates. At Hilo High. Sorry to hear what happened. Good girl, her."

"Where's the boy?" Steamer said.

"Who?"

Ernesto appeared from the legs of the crowd and sat down next to Patsy. Both of them looked up at Steamer.

The cop took a photograph from the clipboard and showed it to Steamer. "You seen this woman around?"

Steamer thought that Antonia looked good in black and white. "What happened over at Papa Joe's?" he asked.

"Looks like Joe caught a couple of guys breaking in. Tried to steal a lot of money. Kinda funny. Never thought Joe had that much money."

Steamer felt small fingers take his hand.

"You seen her around?" the cop asked.

"Who?" asked Mr. Goodmorning. He was standing next to the cop and eating fistfuls of popcorn from a paper bucket.

"This woman?" The cop shook the picture. "Police in Honolulu are looking for her."

"Pretty woman," said Mr. Goodmorning.

"Real pretty," said the cop.

"I'd remember a woman like that," said Mr. Goodmorning. "If I seen her."

The cop nodded. "This da kine too pretty. You have to be careful with this kine. Who's the boy?"

Steamer looked down at Antman. He was standing between Ernesto and Patsy.

"He lives here," Mr. Goodmorning said.

"Mimi's boy?"

Steamer felt Patsy rub against his leg. He remembered Mimi's touch. "Yeah," he said. "Mimi's boy."

The cop bent down and asked, "What's your name, boy?"

"Antman," said the boy.

The cop showed the picture to the boy. "You seen this woman around?"

"Be careful" Mr. Goodmorning said.

"What?" The cop looked up as Patsy reached out and slapped her claw across his hand. "Ouch!!" Shaking his hand, the cop stood up. "It's bleeding."

"Ten pounds," the boy said.

"What?"

"I keep telling people to watch out for that cat," said Papa Joe, walking up and putting his hand on the Steamer's shoulder. "She one crazy cat. Her brother too. Lucky he didn't get his hook claws into you."

"That the one," the cop said, pointing his bleeding hand at Patsy, "got spooky eyes."

"Mimi's cat," Steamer said.

"She's not much on people," Teresa said, standing next to Papa Joe. "Go up to the hospital, Doc Trina take care of that for you."

"Not me," the cop said. "I heard about that place." A black SUV with a red light on top pulled up to the curb, and the bleeding cop jumped in. "You see that woman, give me a call."

"Sure," Said Steamer

"Will do," said Papa Joe.

As the SUV drove off, Teresa said, "Getting tired of cops and black cars. Too many both of them."

Steamer bent down and picked up the picture the cop had dropped on the sidewalk. He looked at Antonia and thought of Mimi. He put the picture in his pocket.

They walked toward the ocean. The boy and Mr. Goodmorning in the lead, Ernesto and Patsy dodging in and out of their legs, dropping back, rubbing against Steamer, waiting for Papa Joe and Teresa.

Steamer found himself in a town at the base of a volcano, on a sidewalk leading to the ocean. How time had passed, he did not know. The sun had burned through misty clouds, created day. He had seen it touch corrugated tin, the narrow streets, the mountain beyond. Where was she now?

Walking against the grain, with two kittens in her mouth, Angelica the Calico passed the boy. Steamer stepped out of her way, and Papa Joe saluted a veteran of the Palace Wars. She was on parade, leaving behind her hiding place in a narrow bed of van Gogh flowers driven mad by the Hilo sun.

Steamer walked with his back to the Palace, toward the horizon that was hidden in darkness. He crossed the street and stopped at the ocean.

He stood on the rocks and watched the skiff makings its way toward Manny's boat. Pulling on the oars, Antonia was almost there. Behind Steamer, the street was quiet, but he felt something moving. If only he could fly upward and see beyond this place, beyond this moment.

They were standing in a line, left to right. "Golden Madonna," Papa Joe said, shaking his head. "Hope that Manny takes care of her."

Teresa crossed herself.

"Man," Mr. Goodmorning said, digging into his bucket of corn. "Wish I knew what to say."

Patsy and Ernesto rubbed against the boy's leg. He was watching his mother go. Steamer rested his hand on the boy's shoulder. He saw a day when they'd be walking the beach, the boy stopping to pick up pieces of worn glass. They'd listen to the waves. They'd smell ginger. Papa Joe would teach the boy how to surf, and Teresa would show him how to swim in the freezing pounds.

"There," Mr. Goodmorning said, pointing at the darkening night. "This is one happy ending!"

They saw the empty skiff drifting, the woman climbing into Manny's boat.

Steamer picked up the boy and held him on this hip. He was a small boy and he was crying. Someday soon, Steamer would sail with him to the breakwater. They would climb the rocks and look out at the endless blue. It would be...

"Going home," said Papa Joe.

Under full sail, Manny's boat reached the breakwater, passed it, and turned into the open ocean. Headed for the horizon, the red boat crossed a sliver of moonlight. Pushed along by the flat surface of increasing humidity, the *Manila Queen* would sail forever on calm seas.

Steamer felt Mimi's touch, her fingers on the edge of his desire. Where was she?

All Pau.

The End.

lz

Glossary of Background and Unfamiliar Terms

Ahi: tasty tuna fish, fresh from the sea, not the kine found in a can.

Arare: salty, crunchy mini-snacks mixed with buttery popcorn for special treat

buggah: undesirable character

coulda: could have

coqui: small very noisy frog that invaded through Kona and spread like maile pilau, except with lots more noise, enough noise so that a TV turned to its highest volume cannot drown out their cries for a mate.

dat: that, as in dis and dat

gotta: have to, got to

friggin: participial form of *frig*

gotta give 'em credit: got to give them credit, a required response from winning coaches when asked about the losing team

hale: house, home, structure

high nose: condescending attitude, as in walking with your nose in the air

Humane Society, According to the *Hawaii Tribune Herald,* (Sunday, June 15, page A12), the

County of Hawaii estimated that whoever took the contract for animal control services on the Big Island "would process 12,800 stray and feral animals annually, plus 3,500 animals turned in by their owners, and adopt out 750 animals, while euthanizing 14,000, about 8,800 on the east side of the island."

kinda: kind of

kine (s): kind, as in da kine, the kind

Kitty Kastle: favored spelling of kitty castle

koi: a type of carp

lotta: lot of

mac salad: macaroni salad, heavy on the mayo

Manny: on his birth certificate Manny's name was spelled *Mani* but he used the more traditional spelling *Manny* so that he wouldn't be confused with Mani, the Gnostic prophet who lived around 210-276 AD and claimed salvation was possible through education and denial of worldly pursuits.

neithers: neither

okole: buttocks, butt, ass, trunk

pakalolo: mood altering plant

maile pilau: informal for stinky vine that covers
everything and stinks when cut

shoulda: should have

thwack: wind up sound plus whack

vog: volcanic smog that stings the eyes and lingers in
the air when the Trade Winds don't blow

Sig Zane: desirable shirt designed in Hilo.

www.ingramcontent.com/pod-product-compliance
Lightning Source LLC
Chambersburg PA
CBHW050503260626
47157CB00004B/1173